PUFFIN BOOKS

Editor: Kaye Webb

THE YOUNG ...... TIVES

Here is .... more than a
s......................kie children
.......................e taken for
.......................ssage leading
...................vas a mysterious in-
.............nd doors too quickly for
r........prints where no footprints should
ha.......n, and a wreck off-shore with something
curious about it too. Here, surely, are all the in-
gredients for a first-rate story. Add that the writing
is good and easy, the pace rapid, and the natural
give and take between the children amusingly true
to life, and you will see for yourselves that this is a
grand book to get down to on a wet day or day in
bed – or any day on which you have not positively
got to go and do anything else; for the probability
is that, once started, wild horses won't get you away
from it till you've finished it.

Mainly for boys and girls from eight or nine upwards.

Cover design by Trevor Stubley

THE
YOUNG DETECTIVES

R. J. McGREGOR

—

ILLUSTRATED
BY
WILLIAM GRIMMOND

PENGUIN BOOKS

Penguin Books Ltd, Harmondsworth, Middlesex, England
Penguin Books Inc., 7110 Ambassador Road, Baltimore, Maryland 21207, U.S.A.
Penguin Books Australia Ltd, Ringwood, Victoria, Australia

—

First published by Burns Oates & Washbourne 1934
Published by Penguin Books 1948
Reprinted 1950, 1952, 1954, 1958, 1961, 1963, 1965, 1967, 1968, 1971, 1972

—

—

Made and printed in Great Britain
by Hunt Barnard Printing Ltd, Aylesbury
Set in Monotype Baskerville

CONTENTS

CHAPTER I

The Mackies Scent Adventure

'Family council, my dears,' said Mrs Mackie, on the first morning of the summer holidays.

'When?' asked the eldest Mackie.

'Immediately after breakfast.'

Family councils were important affairs in the Mackie household and were usually held once or twice every holiday, and the worst punishment one of the children ever had was to be excluded from such a meeting. Daddy never attended these councils; they were private affairs between Mummy and the children, who were quite sure, however, that Mummy always reported the discussions to Daddy afterwards, unless they happened to be concerned with buying his birthday present or something like that.

There were five children in the Mackie family. They were always called the Mackies because that was shorter than Mackenzies. Alan was nearly thirteen and Elizabeth was seven. Jean, David, and Michael came between.

On this particular morning the council was solemnly formed. Mrs Mackie was in the chair, at the head of the long table in the schoolroom. Alan, as the eldest, sat on her right, and Jean opposite to him. David and Elizabeth sat beyond Alan, and Michael next to Jean.

'Now, my dears,' began Mrs Mackie, 'I have something tremendous to say to you.'

'Is it about Daddy going to America?' interrupted Michael.

'Order!' cried Alan. 'Don't you know that you must not speak when the chairman is addressing the meeting?'

'You are speaking yourself,' said David.

'Shut up,' chorused the two girls. 'Go on, Mummy, please.'

'No interruptions, then. Questions can come afterwards. Daddy, as you know, is going to America for a few months on business, but the business that takes him there is a good thing for us in one way, because he has been very well paid to go.'

Michael was just going to interrupt again, but he managed to keep quiet after catching Alan's eye.

'Daddy has bought us a lovely present which he hopes will keep us happy while he is away.'

Mrs Mackie paused and all the Mackies looked at her, bursting with a desire to shout, 'What is it? Tell us at once, quickly, quickly!' But they kept itchily quiet.

'He has bought us a fine old house in Devon. It is in lovely country and near the sea, and has a stream running through the grounds. It is a house with lots of things to make us as happy as can be.'

'Has it a ghost?' asked David, unable to keep quiet any longer.

'Don't be silly,' said Jean. 'Ghosts are only imagination.'

'I saw a ghost once,' declared Michael, 'and it turned out to be the window-curtain blowing half-way across my room. That wasn't imagination.'

'No, and it wasn't a ghost, either,' said Alan.

'The house was partly built as long ago as the time of Henry the Seventh,' Mrs Mackie continued.

'Fourteen eighty-five,' muttered Alan, but the others ignored him. The idea of introducing dates into such a thrilling family discussion was too contemptible to be noticed.

'Since then various owners have added bits to it so that now it is rather a curiosity with about half a dozen different styles of building. In spite of that it doesn't look a bit ugly; in fact, I think it is very fine and beautiful.'

'It must be a big house,' said Jean.

'Yes, it is, huge. That is why Daddy was able to buy it. It was very cheap. We shall only use about half of it.'

'Will there be lots of empty rooms for us to play in?' asked David.

'Yes, and plenty of room out of doors, too.' For the next half an hour Mrs Mackie was bombarded with questions, and after the meeting was ended the children talked it all over among themselves.

They often talked of adventure, but Michael was the only one who truly believed that real adventures could be found by children nowadays. The others, even Elizabeth, were a bit doubtful. They had read many stories of adventures, but, as they said, most of them happened a long time ago or in outlandish places.

'Children like us,' said David, who was very unromantic, 'don't have adventures. We have to go to school, and we play our games, and we go to the Zoo and all that, but you can't call that adventures.'

'Pooh!' replied Michael. 'I heard Daddy say that there's tons of adventure to be had if people have courage.'

'And like to go and look for it,' added Jean. 'I tell you what I think; now that we are going to stop in that lovely old house we might get a big adventure there.'

'Mummy says it's ever so old,' said Elizabeth.

'Yes, and I expect it has rats!' cried David.

'Don't tease,' protested Jean. 'There is no reason why it should have rats.'

'He's only grinning at you,' said Alan. 'We shall soon know all about it. We are going down there next Tuesday, and we shall have six weeks of the place before we have to think of getting ready to go back to school.'

'Yes,' declared Michael, 'and I am going to have an adventure there. You see if I don't.'

'Good man,' laughed Jean. 'I'll help you look for one.'

'Girls don't have adventures; they only spoil other people's,' said David.

Jean and Elizabeth threw cushions at him and he ran away laughing.

'All joking apart,' said Jean, after the uproar had quieted, 'it would be topping if we did have some big adventure in that new house of ours. Suppose we found a treasure or something like that.'

'Yes, suppose,' said Alan. 'It's only about a hundred

million to one against it. No, I'm looking forward to a great time there because – well, I know a secret.'

'It can't be a secret if you know it,' said Elizabeth. 'Unless you made it up.'

'Somebody has to know,' cried Michael. 'Tell us the secret and then it won't be a secret any more.'

'No, I'm not going to, but it has something to do with a horse.'

The others laughed. 'Well, if that isn't telling,' said Michael, 'I don't know what is. Besides, with an old manor house and a horse, if we don't get adventures . . .'

'You've got adventures on the brain. I hope you won't be disappointed, my lad,' said Alan.

'I won't be. You see!'

And see they did.

For the next few days adventure was in the air; they talked about it; they dreamed about it; and each made his or her own secret plans. The whole Mackie imagination was having a Bank Holiday, as Auntie said. The excitement of preparation affected them in various ways, but not one of them knew how to play, eat, or rest.

At last the day arrived. Such piles of luggage were brought down into the hall that Michael declared, almost with tears:

'If all that stuff goes into the car there will be no room for us.'

But he was soon relieved to find that there was to be a hired car as well as their own. After a considerable amount of bother the two cars were loaded. Mrs Mackie drove her own car, with Elizabeth and Michael squeezed into the front seat beside her. The other three children and sundry cases and parcels were in the back.

The second car was driven by a man from a near-by garage, and contained much luggage, and Cook. David said he was thankful Cook was going in the second car.

Jean asked why.

'Because,' he said, 'her weight will probably burst a tyre before they arrive.'

Nora and Edna, the two maids, were coming down by train as soon as they had shut up the house.

The journey took them five hours, including a stop for lunch, and during most of the run Michael swayed backwards and forwards as though urging the car to greater speed. Elizabeth sang softly to herself, 'Boney was a warrior', so many times that it became quite mechanical, and she hardly knew she was doing it.

David yawned his way through two counties! He was very easily bored; even a long drive through the lovely English roads and lanes wearied him.

Mummy hardly spoke all the way. She was a good and careful driver, and had no eyes or thoughts for anything but the road when she had her precious family with her. Alan and Jean chattered more than enough for them all.

Suddenly David's boredom dropped from him like magic.

'Look! The sea!' he cried. 'See the sun shining on it through the gap.'

'Yes,' answered Jean, 'and look at that perfectly marvellous house on the side of the gap.'

For a second Mrs Mackie took her eyes from the road. 'D'you like it?' she asked, softly. There was something in the way she said it that made Jean imperil all their lives by putting her arms round her mother's neck and whispering:

'Mummy . . . it isn't . . . ?'

Mrs Mackie nodded. She was quite unprepared for the wild whoop that Jean let out.

'We shall never get there alive if you do that again, my dear,' she said.

Instantly all the children were peering to get a glimpse again of the wonderful house in its gorgeous setting, but they had turned off the main road and were running between very high hedges which obscured their view.

'How much farther is it, Mummy?' they all wanted to know.

'About twenty minutes' run, my dears; I can't go very quickly here.'

What a long twenty minutes it did seem, but at last they stopped before a big white gate. From a cottage at the side, in answer to the horn, a boy of about Alan's age came running out. He stared at the children and they, in turn, stared at him, as Mummy wrote in her next letter to Daddy, 'like the first meeting of a Chinaman with a tribe of Zulus'.

'Well, John!' called Mrs Mackie. 'Aren't you going to open the gate for us?'

Still staring, he swung open the gate and let them through. He didn't speak a word.

'Who is he?' asked Elizabeth.

'The gardener's boy,' said Mummy.

'Our gardener's?'

'Yes.'

'Have we a gardener all to ourselves down here?'

'Yes, dear, and there is more than enough for him to do.'

All further questions were cut short by their wonderment at what lay in front of them. The house was even more lovely than appeared from a distance, and from the front there was a superb view of sea, cliffs, stretches of sand, big bays, and little coves. The children scrambled out of the car and stood gazing, wondering, and trying to take it all in. David was the first to move. He at once dashed into the house and ran from room to room, upstairs and downstairs; he couldn't move fast enough to see all he wanted to see.

The others followed more slowly, and helped to bring in numerous bits of luggage. Mrs Stallard, the gardener's wife, welcomed them, and said she had a real Devonshire tea waiting for them.

By the time the other car had arrived and its baggage was unloaded, the children had washed, and Mummy had changed her frock, they were all ready to make a hearty raid on the tea. Just as they were sitting down somebody said:

'Where's David?'

They only then realized that nobody had seen him since he had entered the front door.

'Late, as usual,' said Alan.

'Exploring, of course,' added Jean.

'I hope he has not explored too far already,' smiled Mummy. 'We won't wait for him; he'll turn up as soon as he remembers he is hungry.'

Tea was nearly over when he did arrive. He burst into the room.

'Sorry I'm late, Mummy dear,' he said.

'Where have you been and what have you been doing?'

'Coo!' he said. 'Just across one field at the back, there is a pond with heaps of live things in it.'

'Trust him,' laughed Alan. 'You'll have to take up bug-hunting for a living, my lad.'

'I wouldn't mind; I'd go to the Amazon and search for rare orchids and things.'

'Orchids aren't bugs, are they?' asked Michael.

'No, Micky boy, they are caterpillars,' said Jean.

'Don't tease; you know they aren't,' said Elizabeth.

'They are places where apples grow.'

They all laughed at this.

'More unnatural history,' cried Alan.

As soon as tea was over Mrs Mackie said:

'Now I have a great deal of unpacking to do. You can explore until seven o'clock. Don't do anything silly, and be back sharp on time.'

'I'm for the beach,' said Jean. 'Does anybody know the way down?'

'I do,' answered David. 'We have a special way of our own; a private path and steps.'

'How on earth do you know?'

'I saw it just now.'

'Well, lead on then,' cried Alan. 'You seem to have found out a lot in a short time.'

They ran round the lawn, along one side of a rose garden, through a door into another garden with high walls.

'Crumbs!' shouted Michael. 'Look at the fruit!'

'Never mind about fruit,' said Elizabeth, 'we want to get down on the sands.'

13

From the fruit garden they went through another door leading to a flight of mossy steps which descended between walls of rock and ended in a little tunnel, at the far end of which was a gate. When they opened the gate and passed through they found themselves on the cliff. The sands were about a hundred feet below them.

A winding path took them down most of the way. The steepest part was provided with some wooden steps with two ropes for hand-rails.

Eagerly they all scrambled down and rushed to the edge of the sea. Big white-crested rollers were crashing in and running far up the sandy beach. The children ran from rock to rock and from pool to pool. They could not take it all in fast enough. Alan was the first to speak.

'D'you see?' he said. 'No one can get on to this bit of beach except down our private path.'

'Does that mean,' asked David, 'that there will be only ourselves down here?'

Nobody bothered to answer him, so he continued:

'Because, if so, I shan't like it.'

'Don't be a misery,' said Jean. 'Can't you be thankful for once?'

'I know what he means,' said Elizabeth. 'He thinks we always get more fun when there are other children besides ourselves.'

'It will be all right,' replied Michael. 'If we get to know any other children down here we can invite them in to play with us. Mummy won't mind.'

David wasn't listening; he was gazing at the far end of the beach.

'What are you staring at, David?'

'You just watch up there; as the waves go back there is something dark sticking up out of the water. I wonder what it is.'

'There is no need to wonder, then,' called Alan, who was already running in that direction. 'It is a wreck. I expect we could reach it at low water.'

14

They raced along the sandy stretch until they came to a pile of rocks that had fallen from the cliff face. Scrambling and climbing they reached the top and could see quite plainly that it was a wreck. Quite a large steamer had evidently been driven ashore a long time ago, and there she was, partly buried in the sand, with festoons of seaweed hanging from her sides. The waves were dashing over her, and the children could see that they could not possibly approach her at this state of the tide.

'When the tide is out as far as it can go,' said Alan, 'I'm going out to that wreck.'

'I wonder if she has gold in her, like the *Egypt*?' said Micky. 'Wouldn't it be topping to go out and *savage* the gold.'

'I suppose you mean *salvage*,' laughed David. 'It would be topping all right, but I can't imagine much gold being left in a wreck close inshore like that.'

'No, you aren't much of an imaginer,' retorted Micky.

'Anyway, we might play pirates on her,' suggested Jean.

'We've got to get to her first,' said Alan. 'It is a tricky business. We don't want anybody to get washed out to sea and drowned. No, we must wait and watch the tides.'

'You always get very low tides the same days as you get very high ones,' said Elizabeth. 'I learnt that at school.'

David groaned. 'Can't you forget school for a bit?'

'Why should I? I like school.'

'So do I, but this place is so heavenly. . . ' What more David was going to say was cut short by a loud yell from Alan.

'Come here, quick!' he cried. 'Look in this pool between these rocks.'

The other children rushed to see what he had discovered.

'It has gone under there,' he said.

'What has?'

'Such a big one!'

'Such a big WHAT?'

'Fish, you sillies. Look! There he goes! Oh! We're going to have some fun in this place, I know.'

They spent so much time looking for fishes among the rock pools that they hardly noticed how long they had been there. Suddenly Jean glanced at her watch.

'Come on,' she cried. 'We shall have to hurry or we shall be late back.'

'I don't want to go yet,' said Micky.

'I don't suppose any of us do,' replied Alan. 'But seeing we've a perfectly marvellous place like this of our very own, and we can come here every day for the next six weeks, there is no sense in making Mummy cross by being late the very first night.'

They wasted no more time, but scrambled back to the garden as quickly as they could. They found Mrs Mackie talking to the maids, who had just arrived after a very tedious train journey. She welcomed them with an inquiring smile.

'Well dears?' was all she said.

'Oh! Mummy,' they cried, as though with one voice, and then broke into a chorus, very much confused and noisy, of the praises of all the things they had seen.

The mention of the wreck caused an anxious look to come into Mummy's eyes.

'Darlings,' she said. 'You must all promise me one thing. Never attempt to do things which you *know* are silly and too risky.'

'H'm,' said David. 'Daddy says . . . '

Mummy interrupted. 'I know what Daddy says. He doesn't want you to grow up cowards, afraid to take risks, afraid to venture. But there is a lot of difference between being brave and being foolhardy.'

'I was only going to say,' persisted David, 'that Daddy thinks explorers are the world's greatest men, because they dare to go where others have never been.'

'Not just followers, like silly sheep,' added Elizabeth, so quietly that they hardly heard her.

'Yes,' replied Mummy, laughing at their seriousness, 'but you all have enough sense to know when you are doing things that are not brave but merely daft.'

'Oh, Mummy!' teased Jean. 'And only the other day I heard you telling Daddy that it was silly to expect any discretion from kids.'

'What's discretion?' asked Michael.

Mrs Mackie's reply was to the point. 'It is time for your bath and then bed, my son.'

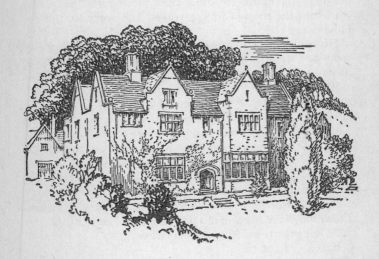

CHAPTER II

Thrilling Discoveries

As Alan lay in his bed that night he could see three winking lights. He tried to time their flashes, but the effort sent him to sleep quicker than usual. He dreamed that they were all imprisoned in the hull of a wreck and that the waves were dashing over them. He could hear the sound of shrieking wind and the thud of furious waves, and woke to find the noises were real.

He could see water streaming down the window of his room and the whole house seemed to be quivering with the fury of the wind.

'Bad start! A wet day,' he grumbled to himself. 'What a rotten business for the beginning of a holiday!'

He jumped from bed and looked out. It was streaming with rain; the trees were bending before the savagery of the wind; the sea looked muddy, and a white crest could be seen on each wave far out to sea. The garden looked swamped, and the clouds were sweeping right across the headland, blotting out all view beyond.

He went into his brothers' room to see if they were awake. They, too, were peering out disgustedly at the weather.

'What's the time, Alan?' asked David.

'Quarter to seven.'

'Then that's all right,' said Michael. 'Rain before seven, fair before eleven. I know that's true, cuz I've proved it.'

'I hope you are right, that's all. I'm going back to bed to read a bit.'

'I'm not,' said David. 'I'm going to get up and do some more exploring.'

'You can't go out exploring this weather.'

'No, but I can explore in the house. There's all that old part at the other end; we haven't looked at that yet.'

'No,' said Alan. 'And for me exploration is a thing to be

done after breakfast, not before. I prefer to explore on a full stomach.'

'Well,' said Micky, 'real explorers often have to starve. Yes, and they still have to struggle on. I've read about them.'

'No doubt, old man. But an explorer who starves when there is a good breakfast being prepared . . . I believe I can smell it . . . is undoubtedly cracked.'

Alan returned to his bed and took with him a volume of *Chums* which he had found in his bedroom. The result was he arrived late to breakfast. He was even after Mrs Mackie, and breakfast was the one function she was never early for.

David and Michael, however, called the girls, and as soon as they were dressed they went on a voyage of discovery. They found the entrance to the old part of the house was locked, but they soon discovered a large key in the kitchen which looked as though it might fit. Fit it did, but it was a terrible struggle to turn it. In the end they were forced to call in Edna's help.

Once the door was opened they entered a long stone-flagged passage, which ran between numerous damp-smelling rooms.

'What a horrible smell!' said Elizabeth.

'I don't think so,' replied Michael.

'Well, it *smells* like a horrid smell, any way,' she declared.

In and out of every room they went, finding nothing to make them very excited. At the end of the passage was a stairway with curious twisty balusters. They raced up the stairs to another long corridor above. Jean was the first to arrive on account of her long legs; she could go up three at a time. As she turned the corner of the stairs at the top she suddenly stopped. The others came rushing up behind her.

David saw her looking slightly scared.

'What's up?' he asked.

After a pause she answered, 'Nothing. I only thought I saw a man go in that room at the end.'

'Mrs Dyke, the gardener's wife, I expect,' said David.

'I said a *man*, fathead! Besides, she went home last night.'

'Well, her husband then. Come on, let's go and see.'

Boldly David led the way, the others backing him up closely. When they reached the door of the room Jean thought she had seen the man enter they hesitated a second.

'Perhaps we ought to knock,' suggested Michael.

Jean gave a loud rap on the door and then threw it open. The children stood close together and peered inside.

'Pooh! Empty!' cried David. 'You and your man! You are seeing things, my child.'

Jean turned on him with scorn. 'Think I'm blind?' she demanded. 'Besides, I'm sure I can smell that someone has been here.'

'Like a bloodhound,' teased David again.

Jean was getting cross. 'Tobacco, idiot! There's quite a smell of it. Some smoky sort of person has been here quite recently.'

Still David persisted in aggravating her.

'Yes, I know what that was. The man you saw has gone up in smoke.'

'All right. I can't prove it because there is nobody here. But I know I'm right.'

'Oh!' cried Michael. 'That's just like a girl . . . '

For a second it almost looked like a quarrel, but Jean cut it short by saying, 'Very well, have it your own way. There is nothing here. Let us look into the other rooms.'

They ran from room to room, finding nothing but emptiness, until they entered the last door they had not tried. They found it led into a short and narrow passage with another door at the end of it. They raced along and soon found themselves in a huge room, that looked like the upper floor of a barn, which was what they afterwards discovered it to be.

'What a topping place to play in!' It seemed as though they all said it together.

It was rather dark in there, so that it was some few

minutes before they made a great discovery. The barn had at some time or other been used for the performance of plays, for across one end of it was quite a good stage.

The children were almost shrieking with delight.

'Now,' cried Jean, 'we shall be able to do our plays decently.'

'Mummy said we always did them well at home,' said Elizabeth.

'She's prejudiced,' replied Michael.

'Don't use big words, Micky boy,' said Jean. 'You can't tell me what prejudiced means.'

'Can't I? Well, when we did our last play and Mummy was so pleased with us and praised us, I heard Cook say, "She's prejudiced," so that's how I know.'

'Yes,' said David. 'Cook rather fancies herself when it's

anything to do with the stage. She goes to the theatre every Saturday night at home.'

'I know,' said Jean. 'Mummy says that's why she is always so flighty and forgetful on Sunday mornings.'

'She gets all worked up,' said Michael, more to himself than to the other children.

'Well,' interrupted David, 'you can get all worked up over this theatre of ours, if you like, but I'm getting all worked down with hunger. If I don't get some breakfast soon I shall start howling like a dog.'

The children all remembered they were hungry then, so they hastened back to the other part of the house. Alan had just come down and they all talked at once in their eagerness to tell him about the barn and the stage. Above all the Mackies he was the one most keen on plays and dressing-up; he could not wait until after breakfast to be shown the great discovery.

'What a treat for wet days!' he cried with enthusiasm. 'We'll fix up a play at once and start rehearsing after breakfast. I wonder if Mummy can lend or make us some curtains. And we'll have to have proper lights. And we could give a performance to the people of the neighbourhood. Oh! this is jolly.'

They all talked at once, each putting forth a fresh idea for a play, each demanding a star part, each deciding on a most suitable costume to wear. Once again it was David who brought them back to earth with a demand for breakfast.

Back they went again. Mummy greeted them with a smile of happiness when she saw how eager they all were. She had to hear all about their great find, too.

'Yes,' she said. 'I knew it was there, although I had not seen it. The gentleman who once owned this house was a famous playwright, and he used to invite actors and actresses to come and spend holidays with him. Then in return for his hospitality they would try out his plays for him.'

'I'm going to write plays when I grow up,' said Jean.

'I hope you will,' said Mrs Mackie, 'but don't forget that

it is one thing to write a play and quite another to get it performed.'

'I should think,' said Alan, 'it would be very jolly just to write them, even if they were never played.'

Breakfast didn't take very long that morning, and as the rain still continued to pour down in a steady torrent they went at once to the theatre, as they already called it.

They spent a good deal of time all talking at once, but in the end it was decided that Alan and Jean should devise a play suitable for them and set about writing the parts at once. The vast number of sheets of paper Jean brought to write on suggested a play of remarkable length.

The other three children wandered about making fresh discoveries, the greatest being a very large box which was full of the most thrilling costumes. David had been wriggling under the stage when he found it, and the three youngest children had a mighty struggle to drag it out. When they opened it and saw what it contained they simply yelled their delight.

Alan and Jean rushed from their play-writing to see what the excitement was about. They joined the others in a mad scramble for the contents of the box, which were hauled out and soon scattered all over the place. The air was full of cries.

'Ah! that'll just do for me.'

'No, you silly, it's too big. I must wear that.'

'No, this is a better one.'

'You'd look a freak in that. I'm darker so it would suit me better.'

'I'm going to have this one, anyway.'

'No, I want it, and I found the box so I ought to have first choice.'

The discovery at the bottom of the box of a Spanish bull-fighter's costume almost led to a quarrel, for they all wanted it, in spite of its being much too big for any of them. It was being tugged and snatched and voices were getting shrill, when Mummy appeared on the scene. She soon restored peace and harmony, and delighted them by promising to help them with the play.

'But,' she said, 'you have all been so busy that you have not noticed the weather. The rain has stopped and the sun is breaking through.'

'What's the time?' asked Micky.

'Nearly eleven.'

'There you are. I told you so. Fair before eleven.'

'Yes,' said Mummy, 'that is very often true. Come on, let us all go out together. I want to go down into the village to see what sort of shops they have there.'

Very soon they were all walking down the lane which led to Oxmouth. The clouds were travelling quickly away, and the sun was so warm that it was making steam rise from the road and hedges. The lane brought them out to a point where they could see the village far below them. The houses and cottages were clustered around a babbling and splashing stream which hurtled over a high ledge of rock and then seemed to lose itself in the sands of the beach.

'That is the stream which runs through our place,' said Mummy.

'Is it?' said David. 'That's funny; I haven't found that stream yet.'

'I thought you couldn't have,' laughed Alan, 'or you would have fallen in it by now.'

Mummy held tight to Elizabeth as they scrambled down the rocky path into the village.

'Is this the only way into Oxmouth?' asked Jean, who was slipping all over the place.

'No, my dear, but the road goes round such a long way that I thought it would be easier to come this way and climb down this path.'

'Huh!' cried David. 'The only thing about climbing down is that you have to climb up again.'

'You needn't,' said Mummy. 'You can go back round the road.'

'How far is it?'

'Only about five miles.'

'Only about . . . Thank you, I'll climb. I prefer it.'

They found the village was not nearly so picturesque at close quarters as it had seemed from the top of the hill. In fact, it was rather squalid, quite dirty, and very smelly.

Elizabeth made a face. 'I don't like the stink of this place,' she said.

'Hush!' said Jean. 'You may offend some of the inhabitants if you speak so loudly. They may object to their native odours being referred to as stinks.'

'Besides,' said Micky, 'it is rather nice; a mixture of tar and rope and fish and sea-weed.'

To show that he at any rate approved he gave a terrific sniff.

'Pooh! he likes it,' said Elizabeth, who was holding her nose.

While Mummy and the girls searched for anything approaching a shop, the boys ran on down to the beach where they could see several boats drawn up and stout, blue-jerseyed fishermen sprawling against them.

'Funny thing,' said Alan. 'At all the seaside places I have been to there are always a crowd of corpulent seafaring men who never appear to do anything more thrilling than lean and lounge against their boats. I suppose they do go out to sea at times, but they always seem to have the knack of looking fat and comfortable on nothing at all.'

'I expect it is the sea air,' said Michael.

'Or the smells,' added David.

They scrambled about among the boats and spoke to some of the men; were invited by several to go for a sail for 'just 'arf a dollar. Take the lot of yer'; stopped to watch an artist who was painting, 'something lovely', as Micky expressed it; and finally had a tremendous thrill by discovering that Oxmouth had a lifeboat. The house was open and a few visitors were walking round the boat, climbing up a ladder to look inside it, and asking silly questions of a very patient old sailor with one leg, who seemed to find great pleasure in splashing buckets of water about.

Just as they were leaving the lifeboat house Alan let out a wild whoop of joy, for they walked right into Jerry Walton, a boy from his own house at school.

After scores of questions from both sides they found that Jerry was stopping at a farm close to Oxmouth, and was to be there for a whole month.

'Then you'll be able to come over to our place. Here is my mater coming; she'll invite you, I know.'

Mrs Mackie was pleased to meet Alan's friend, and promptly asked him to come over to tea that same day. He dashed off to find his mother, and Alan called after him, 'Bring your bathing things.'

After frantic whisperings from Alan, Mrs Mackie went to the most alert-looking of the boatmen and bargained with him for the hire of himself and his boat for one or two days a week when the weather was fine enough for the children to go out in safety. He agreed to bring the boat round to their own beach the following morning, and seemed very pleased when he knew it was the people from 'the big house' he was dealing with.

'Glad to know the place is occupied again,' he said. 'It has been empty so long we began to feel we never should have anybody there again.'

In some mysterious way the news that they were the new family up at the Manor spread like lightning, for as they went back through the village they were aware that scores of pairs of eyes were watching them from behind window curtains and through cracks of doors.

Mummy was rather silent as they walked home. Alan was with her, and the others were scattered about chasing butterflies, or picking flowers from the hedges.

'What's the matter, Mummy?' he asked at last.

'Matter, my son? Nothing.'

'But you are so very quiet.'

'I was just thinking.'

'About Daddy?'

'Yes, and other things.'

'I wish he was with us.'

'Yes, so do I. His going away has given us the money to have these lovely things and he is not here to enjoy them with us.'

'But he'll come back?'

'Oh! yes, dear; but I was puzzling over something else.'

'Not worried, are you, Mummy?'

'Not exactly. But did you notice anything about those people down in the village?'

'I didn't think they seemed too friendly.'

'Ah! you noticed it, did you? Then it wasn't my fancy. I am wondering what it meant.'

'Just natural suspicion of strangers, I expect.'

'No, I don't think it can be that, for they have to earn a great deal of their living from strangers who come down during the summer months for holidays.'

'I wonder . . . ' Alan paused.

'Well?'

'Perhaps it is silly.'

Mummy gave his hand a loving squeeze. 'And very likely it isn't. Tell me what you were going to say.'

'Well, I wonder if they resent us . . . or anybody . . . being at the old house. You see, we are outsiders to them. Probably they were very attached to some ancient family who lived there always.'

'That may be it, but I have an idea it is something else as well. There is no knowing how much the villagers have had the run of our property while it was empty so long.'

'The fisherman seemed quite pleased to know that we were there.'

'True. But I noticed something else. His name is Maclean, and he does not speak like a man of these parts, so he may regard us differently from the others.'

They all arrived back at the house, hot, tired, and hungry.

They had their meal, and then Mummy insisted on their resting until Jerry came, before they went to bathe.

During the resting time Alan and Jean wrote some more of the play while the others read. Mummy helped the writers with some ideas, and suggested they might have Jerry in as one of the characters.

'Why not the gardener's boy, too?' suggested Elizabeth.

'I shouldn't object,' said Mummy, 'but I expect he would be rather shy. It is difficult to get a word out of him at any time.'

'He can be call-boy,' said Michael.

'We shall want an electrician,' said Alan.

'Really!' exclaimed Mummy. 'Perhaps you would like me to have a revolving stage built for you.'

'Thank you for the suggestion,' said Alan, laughing. 'But seriously, Mummy, it would be safer than lamps and candles and things if we could have a lead taken in there from our house supply of electricity.'

'I'll see what it would cost. But please don't run away with the idea that we are millionaires.'

Jerry arrived when they were all getting very impatient for his coming. He explained that he would have been there earlier, but he had missed his way.

At once they prepared for their swim. Mummy came, too, and they were proud to show Jerry what a fine place they had.

'This is perfectly ripping!' he cried.

The tide was rather far out and they at once made for the direction of the wreck. There was a good sandy floor, but the waves were rather boisterous, so Mrs Mackie would not let them go far.

'Wait,' she said, 'for a calmer day and a lower tide.'

So they had to be content. The swimming was fine and they had brought a couple of boards with them for surf-riding, so they had a perfectly glorious afternoon.

CHAPTER III

Imprisoned in a Wreck

THAT evening, after the three youngest of the Mackies had gone to bed, Alan and Jean walked across the fields to show Jerry the easiest way home. After they had left him and were returning, they talked over many things about the holiday, the house, the play, until they drew near the little bridge over the stream behind their house.

Here Alan stopped and pointed. 'That,' he said, 'must be the barn. Let us go and have a look at it.'

They were just starting to run to the old wing where the great barn was when Jean stopped suddenly.

'Wait,' she said. 'D'you see that man going across towards the farm?'

'What about him?' asked Alan.

'I'm sure that's the man I saw this morning.'

'Man? What man? What are you talking about?'

'I forgot. You weren't there. When we first went into the old part of the house this morning I was the first upstairs. Just as I reached the top I saw a man go into a room at the end of the corridor. We all went to the room to look for him, but there was no one there. David poked fun at me and said I imagined it.'

'If he wasn't there you must have imagined it.'

'I didn't, I tell you. And that is the man, going across there. I am sure of it. I didn't say too much to the kids about it this morning because I did not want to frighten them.'

'Did you tell Mummy about it?'

'No, in the excitement of other things I forgot all about it.'

'Well, don't say anything about it. We'll do a little detective work on our own. If that fellow is mucking about in our house when he has no business there we shall have to keep a watch on him. It will be jolly to do a little sleuthing.'

They had supper with Mummy, and she allowed them to

stay up afterwards to talk to her and to do a bit more to the play. Just as Mrs Mackie warned them that it was time for bed, Alan suddenly remembered something.

'Mummy,' he said. 'Before we left home you said something about us having a horse to ride.'

Mrs Mackie laughed. 'I've been wondering all day when that question was coming. I've been most astonished that you have not thought of it before.'

'Well, we have hardly been here a day and we have seen and done such crowds of things that there was no time to think of it.'

Alan sat on the arm of his mother's chair and put his arm about her. 'When can I see the horse?' he asked.

'A man from the farm is bringing it round in the morning, if it is fine. He will take you for a ride before breakfast.'

'Can't I go too?' asked Jean.

'Not tomorrow. You must take it in turns until I am satisfied that you are safe to be trusted out alone. Then we will arrange how you are to share him.'

They kissed Mrs Mackie good night and then went off to bed.

All the children were up at what Cook called a 'blessed-unearthly' hour the next morning, especially when they went to the kitchen and bothered her for something to eat before they went out. Jean and the three young ones were for the beach, for they knew there was to be a very high tide at about half past eight. They had seen a tide table in the village.

Alan was waiting impatiently for the man with his horse. Soon he saw him coming up the drive, riding a huge black horse and leading a smaller brown one.

Jean excitedly clutched Alan's sleeve and whispered, 'It is the same man. You know, the one we saw last night.'

He did not answer; he was too thrilled at the sight of the lovely creature he was going to ride.

The man slid from his saddle and touched his cap to Alan. 'Morning, sir,' he said, in the pleasantest of voices.

There was a chorus of praise from all the children, and

they all wanted to smooth and pat the horses, but the man warned them that they were a bit impatient as neither of them had been ridden for some time. He helped Alan to mount and put his stirrups right for him, and they started off to the accompaniment of cheers from the family.

Jean and the others turned about and hurried down to the rocks, where they did little but watch huge waves come dashing in, giving them showers of spray.

Breakfast time found them all ravenously hungry and Mummy said how pleased she was to see them all so ready to eat. Alan was eager to tell them about his ride.

'The man's name is Stidson,' he said, 'and he seems quite a decent chap. He took me up over that piece of moor that you can see the other side of the main road, and he let me gallop.'

'Didn't you fall off?' asked Elizabeth.

Alan looked at her with great scorn, but did not answer.

'No,' said David, 'he clutched the pony round the neck.'

'You wait,' said Alan.

'When I go out on the pony I shall wear that cowboy costume we found in the dressing-up box.'

Michael's remark brought forth a howl of derision from the other children which made him blush. He was beginning to look angry when Mummy smoothed things over by saying:

'You would look lovely in it, darling, but don't you think it would be a wee bit too big?'

'That wouldn't matter.'

'Perhaps,' laughed David, 'it would be an advantage. You see, the trouser legs would be long enough to tie underneath the pony's belly, so Micky wouldn't fall off.'

'All right, you can laugh,' said Michael. 'But don't forget that last holidays you wore a pair of Daddy's riding-breeches.'

'Yes, and he cried because Auntie wouldn't let him go to the Zoo in them.'

'Cried, did I?' demanded David. 'I'm sure I didn't.'

Mummy thought it was time to interrupt again.

'I think,' she said, 'we'll say like they do in the newspapers: this discussion is now closed. I have a plan to put before you.'

'Carried unanimously!' cried Alan.

'Wait until you know what it is.'

'Oh, we all know that something good is coming when you speak like that, so you need not trouble to put it to the vote.'

'Speak for yourself,' said David. 'Let us hear what it is, first.'

'Don't be a pig,' cried Jean. 'You know Mummy's ideas of a treat are always first-class.'

'I know, but I thought she had a look in her eye that might have meant that she was going to pull our legs.'

Mrs Mackie laughed. 'No, no leg-pulling this time.'

'Tell us, then, quickly,' demanded Elizabeth.

'Well, it's just this. I thought we might spend the whole day out, seeing it is so beautifully fine and warm. We can take our lunch. The tide will be out a very long way about two o'clock and we might manage to reach the wreck. Then tonight's tide is the highest for a long time, and I thought we should enjoy watching it come right in.'

'Carried *nem. con.*,' said Jean. 'I don't know what it means, but I've heard Daddy say it.'

'Don't use words you don't know the meaning of,' said Michael. 'It's very ig . . . igno . . . '

They all waited for him to get the word out.

'Very ignominous.'

'Quite!' said Alan; 'very!'

'And what do you mean by ignominous?' asked David.

'You know, what Jean is.'

Mummy could see that more teasing was coming, so she thought the best thing she could do was to set all the children busy making preparations for a long day out. Soon everybody was busy; collecting bathing costumes, preparing very home-made fishing tackle, packing grub into baskets, searching for a bat and ball for beach cricket, and putting ready far more luggage than they could possibly carry.

Mrs Mackie's wants were very few; a rug to sit on, a book to read, a pair of binoculars, and her camera.

'Aren't you going to bathe, Mummy?' asked Elizabeth.

'No,' said Mummy, 'I would rather have a lazy day today; I just want to bask in the sun, read my book, and watch my children enjoying themselves.'

There was endless running about before they had everything ready, and then they made quite a procession down to the sands. They left a message that if Jerry came he was to be sent down to look for them.

'I hope he will come,' said Alan. 'I ought to have told him to come when he liked. You wouldn't mind, Mummy?'

'I thought of what you didn't,' she replied, 'so I expect he will be here quite soon.'

They had barely started when they heard a shout behind them, and there he was chasing after them.

The morning, or what was left of it, was spent in very excited and noisy attempts to catch little fish in the rocky pools. Michael planned the construction of a special fishpond of their own in a sheltered spot between a circle of rocks. Alan told him it would require an army of navvies, two or three steam excavators, and about three thousand tons of cement!

'Well, we shouldn't have to pay for the sand, anyway,' remarked Elizabeth.

Every few minutes they were looking out to sea to estimate the amount the tide had retreated, and how much of the wreck was uncovered. They were so anxious about it that Mrs Mackie let them have their lunch quite early so that they could have a rest before going into the water.

At last they were allowed to start. Clad only in their bathing clothes they dashed off, Alan and Jerry leading, with Jean a very good second. They ran out over the hard firm sand, 'beautifully water-waved', as Jean said, and then splashed through the little ripples. The water round about the wreck was only up to Elizabeth's waist, so they all felt quite safe.

Suddenly there was a loud yell from David. They turned to see what was the matter. A vigorous turmoil in the water showed where Michael had plunged unexpectedly into a deep pool.

They fished him out, and in less than ten seconds he had disappeared into another one. This time, while Alan and

Jerry were grabbing for him, they, too, found themselves in deep water. There was much shouting and excitement, and not a little nervousness before they were all on a safe spot again.

'This won't do,' said Alan. 'I can see what it is; the tide swirling round the sides of the wreck has scoured a deep channel. We must try to get round to the other side over that big rock.'

Carefully holding hands in a long line, with Alan leading and Jerry bringing up the rear, they waded round to the far side of the wreck where it was wedged against a rock. They then saw that it would be almost impossible for them to climb up the deck because her sides were all green and slimy. Seaweed was growing around her, too.

'A fair-sized steamer,' said Jerry. '*Carolina* I see she is called. I wonder how she came to run ashore in a place like this.'

David, as usual, was the first to find out that a hole had been cut in the side of the ship at some time or other.

'Here you are,' he shouted, 'we can get right inside this way.'

They all scrambled through the hole and then stopped short. It was rather dark in the hold of the ship, and there was a good deal of sand, water, and seaweed about. It didn't look very inviting and not nearly so thrilling as they expected.

'Can't we get on to the deck?' asked Jean, who was nosing around a little more venturesomely than the boys. 'That's what I want to do, and then we can have her for our private ship.'

'Looks to me,' said Alan, 'that all the insides have been taken away. There are no engines; in fact, nothing but an empty hulk.'

'Didn't you see that the hole we came through had been cut out?' replied Jerry. 'Several plates had been removed. The hole that sunk the ship is not that one. No doubt all that was of any use in her has been taken out. They always do that if it is possible, even though they may not be able to save the whole ship.'

'Here you are,' cried David again. 'There is a way up to the deck. Here is an iron ladder.'

Their eyes were now getting more used to the poor light, and they saw that what he said was true, so quickly they began to scramble up. Not until they were all on it did someone say:

'I suppose it's safe.'

Elizabeth clutched the ladder very tightly as she went up and felt a bit nervous about it, but soon they were all safely up. They found the deck so slippery that they could hardly stand on it, and running about was impossible. Holding on wherever possible they managed to go right round the ship. Alan climbed on to what was left of the bridge and waved wildly to Mrs Mackie, whom he could see walking out in their direction.

When she saw him she waved and signalled to him that they should return. He made a trumpet out of his hands and bellowed back to her that they were all quite safe. She could not hear what he was saying, but once again waved them back.

After they had played about for some while, Alan came down from the bridge, and said, 'Mummy's calling to us to come back; I think she is a bit nervous about us.'

'Perhaps she thinks the tide may come back with a rush and trap us,' said Micky.

'No danger of that,' replied Jerry. 'At any rate, not if we keep our eyes open.'

'Anyway, I am going back and taking Libby with me,' said Jean.

'Don't call me Libby,' snapped Elizabeth.

'Call her Tin Liz instead,' said Michael, grinning.

Jean went down the ladder first, helping her sister rung by rung, and they were both very relieved when they arrived at the bottom. Just as they reached the hole in the side of the ship quite a big wave came washing through and swamped them.

'Hey! You boys!' shouted Jean up the ladder. 'The tide is coming back. You had better hurry or you will be cut off.'

As the water ebbed out of the side again the girls ran out, but once again a wave came and nearly took them off their feet. They both became rather alarmed and shouted lustily to the boys, who looked over the side to see what they wanted.

'We shall be cut off if we don't hurry,' Jean called.

'Rubbish!' said David. 'The tide takes hours to come in.'

'All right, we're going. Come on, Jean,' replied Elizabeth. 'You'll all be drowned, and it will serve you right.'

'Ta-ta, my little fairy!' cried Micky.

They turned and set off for safety. They had to climb back over the big rock again, and when they reached the other side they were both really alarmed. The water was rushing round it in an angry kind of way.

'Do you think you can get through there if I hold on to you tight?' said Jean.

'No,' answered Elizabeth, in a shaky kind of voice. 'Oh! I wish the boys would come.'

'Stay there, then, and I will go back and tell them they must come.'

'Do hurry. Look, there's another huge wave gone right round us.'

'Righto! Sit still. I won't be two secs.' Jean spoke more cheerfully than she felt, as she once again turned back to warn the boys. She stood at the top of the rock and called with all the power of her voice. Something in her tone stirred Alan and he immediately called to the others.

'Coming,' he yelled, and drove David and Michael down the ladder. In a few seconds they were down and he and Jerry followed. At the bottom David's sharp eyes spotted something which attracted his attention.

'What's this?' he cried.

'Come on, we can't waste time,' shouted Jerry.

'But do look, just one second. This can't have been in the wreck very long. It looks quite new.'

'What is it?' asked Alan, interested in spite of his hurry to get away.

'A box or chest of some kind, and it's got a decent lock on it.'

They all clustered round to examine it as well as they could. They agreed that it could not have been in the water very long. Then David made a new discovery.

'Look,' he said. 'It is weighted down with these lumps of stone. See, ropes have been threaded through the handles at the end and tied to these bits of rock.'

'Funny,' said Jerry. 'I wonder what's inside.'

They tried to lift the lid but could not budge it.

'Locked, of course,' said Alan. 'I can't understand what it can be doing here.'

They wasted so much time wondering about the box that they forgot the danger they were in until an extra big wave came into the hold with a roar and a hiss.

'This won't do. We have got to go.' So saying, Alan led the way out. They had to wade through deep water to reach the rock on which Jean was now almost weeping with anxiety. When they had all reached the top one glance was enough to tell them they had wasted too much time.

'If we aren't cut off,' said Alan, 'we very soon shall be.'

'I'm a good swimmer. Let me see if I can get across,' said Jerry.

'If you can it does not follow that the rest of us can.'

Jerry did not listen to Jean's protest but lowered himself into the water and waded out a little way. Almost at once, a strong wave took him off his feet and as it retreated sucked him back in a way that made the young ones cry out with terror. But he had not been boasting when he said he was a good swimmer, and after a brief struggle he was up on the rock again.

'No, some of us might do it with luck,' he said, 'but it is too risky for the others. Our safest plan is to climb back to the wreck again and wave to your mother and let her see the fix we are in.'

'Poor Mummy,' said Elizabeth. 'She will be scared.'

'I think it is poor us,' said Michael. 'Nobody would have expected the beastly tide to come back so soon.'

'I expect we ought to have come out a bit earlier,' answered

Jean. 'But it is no use talking; we are in a nasty situation and we must try to make ourselves safe until we are rescued.'

It was a brave speech for Jean to make, for she was really very frightened. She seemed to realize their danger more than the others, but she would not add to their troubles by making them unnecessarily frightened.

'Then the best thing,' agreed Alan, 'will be to get back to the wreck and climb up as high as possible. The tide never covers it completely.'

'No, but the waves were dashing right over it this morning when we came down early.'

'Don't be a pessimist, David,' said Jean, taking Elizabeth by the hand and leading the way. 'Mummy will soon see, if she has not done so already, that we must be rescued. She'll send a boat or something.'

'I wish they would send the lifeboat from Oxmouth,' said Michael.

'Yes, and then there would be a picture in the paper. You know, "Oxmouth lifeboat rescues party of children from wreck on South Coast." We should all be interviewed.'

'If you are rescued, David, by a smelly boat all littered up with bait and fishing tackle you'll be lucky. And the man will want to be paid well for his trouble,' said Alan.

It did not take them long to get back to the deck of the *Carolina* again, and they huddled on the bridge and shouted together and waved frantically to Mrs Mackie, who was standing at the edge of the onrushing tide peering through her glasses, which she had brought to look for passing ships.

'What can Mummy be looking at?' said Michael. 'She is not looking this way at all. Let us give a great yell again.'

'Shipwrecked mariners,' said David, 'usually try to attract attention by tying a shirt to a spar, but as we haven't a shirt between us, and certainly nothing to rig up as a mast ...'

'Couldn't we make a raft?' interrupted Michael.

'We could,' replied Alan, 'if there was any woodwork left on this ship and we had a useful box of tools to use.'

At that moment an unusually big wave hit the side of the *Carolina* and made her quiver right through.

'Gosh!' said Jerry. 'A few more batterings like that and anything might happen.'

'She's been battered by winter storms for eleven years, old man,' said Alan. 'It will take more than these waves to shift her.'

Once again they called to Mummy, but to their amazement she did not move or look in their direction, but kept staring through her glasses away to her right.

'We're in a rotten fix,' said David.

They all became very silent until Elizabeth let out a loud yell.

'Look!' she cried. 'That is what Mummy has been watching all the time.'

CHAPTER IV

Rescue

AT once every head turned as though worked by some mechanical contrivance. There was a pause of a very few seconds, and then with one voice they shouted, 'A boat!'

They waved their arms frantically as though they must attract the attention of the boatman, although it was obvious that he was coming directly towards them. They cheered lustily and danced with excitement and relief. They all pretended to be very brave, and affirmed very boldly, now that the danger appeared to be past, that they had not really been nervous, and that they knew they were bound to be rescued in time.

'We really are shipwrecked mariners,' said Michael, with a real thrill of pride.

'I wish it had been the lifeboat,' added David. 'It would have seemed more real.'

'Well,' said Jerry, 'I think it has been very real. If that boat had not appeared we might have been in a very unpleasant situation indeed.'

'Never mind about "ifs",' replied Jean. 'Daddy says that "if" men never get anywhere.'

'Yet you're always saying it yourself,' said David.

'Well, I'm not a man, am I?'

'Shut up,' cried Alan. 'I believe the boat that is coming over is ours. I think I can recognize the man Mummy hired it from yesterday.'

It took a much longer time than they anticipated for the boat to come near enough for the man to hail them.

'Hullo!' he called. 'You're marooned, are you?'

'Come and take us off,' shouted Alan. 'We are getting cold. We have been here long enough.'

'You must wait a bit,' he replied. 'It isn't so easy to bring a boat alongside with all these waves banging her about. I must let the tide get a bit higher yet. Do you know how to fasten a rope securely?'

There was a scornful chorus of 'Yes' in reply.

'We can all do knots.'

'Right! As soon as I can work round the big rock I will come alongside the bow and I shall throw a rope. See that you make it very secure.'

The next half hour passed pleasantly enough. They had no worry about getting off safely, so they explored the ship quite thoroughly. Alan warned all the others not to say a word to the boatman about the box they had found in the hold. They were curious to know why, but at first he would not give a reason.

'Just because . . . ' he said.

'That's no reason,' argued David.

'It's enough reason for you, old son.'

'Then I shall tell him.'

'No, don't. Promise you won't and then when we get home I'll tell you my reasons.'

They all agreed to that, and gave their attention once more to the boatman's efforts to bring himself alongside. Three times it looked as if he had succeeded when a strongly rising wave caused him to pull out again.

At last he was able to run in on a patch of slack water and hug the side of the *Carolina*. At the same instant he cleverly threw a line which the boys all grabbed at, and missed.

'Look out and hold fast this time,' he called, as he threw again.

The coil of rope curled itself about them in such a way that they could not have missed it if they had tried. With eager haste they made it fast and the sailor ran his end through an iron ring in the bow of his boat and tied it securely. His boat-hook he used to keep her steady, and to prevent her beating herself alongside.

'Now,' he said. 'If you two bigger boys can drop over the side first I can see about getting the others off.'

Without waiting for another word Jerry dived over and was soon bobbing up at the stern of the boat. He struggled aboard and then, when the *Kitty*, as she was called, rose on the next wave Alan jumped. He hurt his toe and nearly pitched over into the sea, but after a minute he was hanging on to the boat-hook with Jerry trying to keep the boat close to the side of the *Carolina* when she tried to pull away, and also struggling to keep her off when she seemed intent on banging herself to bits.

Maclean, the boatman, stood up and balanced himself as only a sailor can.

'The little girl first,' he said.

Elizabeth answered in a nervous voice, 'What do you want me to do?'

'Climb over that rail and hold tight. Then, when I say "Jump," jump quickly. I'll catch you. You'll be quite safe. I won't let you fall.'

Elizabeth did as she was told, and as the *Kitty* was rising on a big wave Maclean shouted, 'Now!'

Without hesitating she leapt outwards and the man caught her easily and set her down in the boat.

'Splendid!' he cried. 'That was plucky. Now the other girl.'

'Let me be last,' said Jean.

'Are you afraid?'

'No, but . . .'

'Come on; don't be a coward.'

Jean hated the suggestion that she might be a coward, so without waiting for the word she jumped. Of course she jumped at the wrong moment, when the *Kitty* was at the bottom of a wave instead of the top. The result was disastrous. Jean was the heaviest child of them all, and she landed on Maclean so awkwardly that she knocked him backwards and the gunwale of the boat caught him behind the knees. In one second they were both struggling in the water.

Shrieks from the children didn't help matters. Alan and Jerry both dropped the boat-hook simultaneously, and endangered all their lives by letting the *Kitty* swing free. Fortunately Maclean was both a very strong man and an expert swimmer. He soon calmed everybody and ordered the boys to hold the boat steady again. As soon as they did so he helped Jean aboard and then hauled himself in.

'You are all wet,' said Elizabeth, pointing to the boatman's dripping garments.

'What else do you expect?' answered Jean, snappily. She had swallowed some sea-water and she had been very frightened, so she was not feeling very sweet. Elizabeth annoyed her still further by adding, 'It was your silly fault. You jumped too soon.'

'Oh, yes! You, of course, did it beautifully.'

'So she did,' put in Maclean. 'But we are none of us any the worse, so there is no need to quarrel. It isn't the first time I have gone overboard with all my clothes on.'

He had taken off his coat and now stood up and called to Micky. 'Now, son, jump when I call, and not till then. But don't hesitate. Now!'

Micky jumped well, and was soon laughing beside Elizabeth. Then came David's turn, which was also safely accomplished.

'You see,' he said. 'The captain is always the last to leave his ship.'

'Pooh!' said Jean, who was still feeling a little sore, 'if you were a decent captain you would go down with your ship.'

'Yes, and you must have been a rotten bad captain to run your ship aground,' laughed Jerry.

Maclean grinned quietly to himself. This sort of leg-pulling was new to him, but he was quite capable of entering into the game. Raising his hand in a nautical style, he said:

'Now, sir, what course had we better steer? I think I can see land over there. I hope the natives are not hostile.'

Very solemnly David answered, 'The queen of these parts is well known to me. I am sure she will give us right welcome.'

'What sort of a welcome is right welcome?' asked Alan.

'A right-handed welcome with a stick in it, I should think,' said Maclean. 'Don't forget that a captain who loses his ship has to answer a Board of Trade inquiry.'

'Then I shall remain with the queen of this country,' replied David. 'As I said, I am sure she will give me welcome.'

'You said "right welcome",' began Elizabeth.

'Give way, my hearties,' he interrupted. 'There will be a royal feast awaiting us.'

'A right royal feast, you mean,' laughed Alan.

So chipping and teasing one another, they rowed in towards shore. By the time Maclean had skilfully grounded the *Kitty* in a little sand channel, good-humour was fully restored and the danger of their adventure had been forgotten. They tumbled out of the boat and overwhelmed Mrs Mackie with their various accounts of what had taken place, every one speaking at once.

Alan, as soon as he had an opportunity, put his arm through hers and led her away from the others.

'Were you terribly worried about us?'

Mrs Mackie smiled. 'Not a bit,' she said.

'Then you didn't realize the danger we were in?'

'Yes I did, but you see, I had taken my precautions.'

'How?'

'I had sent a message to Maclean that he was to bring the *Kitty* round as soon after low water as possible, and to come by the wreck in case of accidents.'

'Then it wasn't just a lucky chance that he came that way when he did.'

'I am not much of a believer in "just a lucky chance", my son. Things happen to us because of what we do, or what others do. All the same I think you all ought to be careful to thank the boatman decently for what he did.'

'Isn't it you we have to thank, for taking such careful thought?'

'A little, perhaps. But just imagine what might have happened if he had not done his part. He kept his word to come round at low water. Suppose he had failed!'

'Don't talk about it,' said Alan.

'No, all's well. Let us see about a first-class tea now.'

By the time they had put some clothes on and helped the man haul the boat up above the reach of the tide, they were more than ready for the tea, and it was, indeed, first-class.

Maclean was invited to have it with them, but he excused himself by saying he must really get out of his wet things. Before he went Alan very much astonished him by shaking his hand and saying, 'Thank you for saving our lives.'

'I don't know about that, sir,' he said.

'We know,' said Mrs Mackie, 'and we are not likely to forget.'

'Three cheers for the lifeboat crew,' cried Jean, and they all stood up and gave Maclean a very hearty shout, sending him away smiling happily.

After tea and a game of cricket on the sands the tide drove them up the cliff, where they stayed watching the beauty and majesty of the waves.

'Isn't it wonderful?' said Mummy.

'Especially seen from a safe distance,' replied Jean.

'Yes,' added Elizabeth. 'When you are down among the waves, and you think you are cut off and you have no idea how you can possibly be saved, the waves seem terrifying.'

'You'll have bad dreams tonight, Libby,' said David.

'DON'T call me Libby. And I am no more likely to have bad dreams than you. It was all your fault we got cut off by the tide.'

'How do you make that out?'

'If you hadn't found that box in the hold,' said Jerry, 'we should probably have got away in time.'

'And then we should not have had the fun of being rescued,' said Michael.

'FUN!' almost shouted Jean, 'there wasn't much fun about it.'

Jerry laughed quietly. 'I thought it was awfully funny to see the way you landed on top of the boatman and knocked him flat over the side.'

'Jean's weight again,' said David.

'What box are you talking about?' demanded Mummy.

They all started to tell her at once, but after a time she was able to make head and tail of the story.

'I expect,' she said, and then stopped.

'Expect what, Mummy?' It was Jean who spoke.

'Nothing,' she said.

There was a loud chorus of protest at that. 'You can be tantalizing when you like, can't you?' said Alan.

'All women are like that,' said David. 'Girls are, anyway, and women are only girls got bigger.'

He jumped up and ran away laughing. Elizabeth called after him, 'Boys are stupid!', but the remark was quite wasted, because he didn't hear it.

When they arrived back at the house they were delighted to find a long letter from Daddy for Mummy and postcards for all the children. He said that so far most of his time in America was taken up in being taken to various people's homes and clubs and shown off, as he said, 'like the prize bull at the Royal Show'.

The next few days passed in riding, bathing, boating, fishing, cricket, exploring rocks and caves, and having the greatest time of their lives. At the end of their first week Auntie Frances, Daddy's sister, arrived. The children were all very fond of her, for she had done a tremendous lot for them, and she had kept house for Daddy during the winter that Mummy had spent in India.

They welcomed her noisily, but their noise became deafening when they had discovered she had brought Chris with her.

Chris was Mummy's dog, a wire-haired terrier. He had been left behind at a vet's when they left home because he had been suffering from a nasty wound, the result of a one-sided argument with a strange cat which had invaded their garden.

His full name was Cotham Christopher Strong, and the Mackies were always ready to tell anybody how he was given his name. Being quite a gentleman born he took the name of the kennel from which he came. All the best dogs from his original home were called Cotham something-or-other. The Christopher Strong part of it came about like this.

Mummy brought him home, a perfectly darling puppy ten weeks old. Of course, the first thing the children demanded was:

'What are you going to call him, Mummy?'

'We shall have to think of a name,' Mrs Mackie had replied.

'I know,' said Daddy. 'Call him after the name of this book I am reading. Jolly fine book, jolly fine dog.'

The name of the book was *Christopher Strong*, and so they called him. His name is in the register at the Kennel Club, Cotham Christopher Strong, but nobody ever calls him anything but Chris.

After Chris had gone nearly mad with excitement and had jumped over them all, and licked every part of them he could reach, and Mummy had hugged him, he rushed off to do his own exploring. Within two minutes there was a tremendous barking from the kitchen.

'He's found the cat,' said Mummy. 'Run and bring him back.'

Alan went to find him, and there he was, quivering with eagerness to get at the cat, which had fled to the top shelf of the dresser.

'Take him away,' demanded Cook, 'that blessed cat'll have all them blessed dishes down in a minute. He ran right under my blessed feet and nearly threw me on the blessed floor.'

'That would have been a blessed business,' laughed Alan.

It was a standing joke in the Mackie household that Cook's one and only adjective of any force was 'blessed'. They themselves were usually referred to as 'them blessed children'.

Auntie was as thrilled as the rest of them with the new house, although she had seen it before. She had been down with Mummy and Daddy when they had first thought of buying it. She threw herself into all the enjoyment of the jolly things the Mackies were doing, and promised to help in any way she could with the play.

'Auntie could type out all our parts for us,' suggested Micky.

'Laziness,' said Mummy. 'You must all write out your own parts. It will help you to learn your lines.'

Another wet day drove on the preparations for the play fast. Mummy had found a very handy man from the village who could do a bit of carpentering and electric wiring. Curtains and lights were fixed and the stage began to look quite professional.

The actual writing of the play was more Jean's effort than anybody's, although Alan made a good many suggestions, and Mummy put it into shape for them.

Rehearsals began under difficulties. Elizabeth was the only member of the cast who knew her part properly, but as her principal duty was to be 'invisible voices', as Micky described them, she had not so much to learn as the others.

David didn't know even his first line, and when the others threatened to turn him out of the play if he did not try to get his part off by heart quickly, he said he didn't care.

Auntie smoothed over this difficulty by keeping him with her and rehearsing his part with him until he knew it quite as well as the rest.

For a week their outdoor activities were cut short in order to get the play perfect. It had been decided that they should invite as many people as cared to come, or as many as the barn would hold.

Mrs Mackie encouraged them to do the play really well.

'I shall be quite pleased,' she said, 'for people to come and see you perform your own play, but I shall insist on your doing the thing properly. You shall not give a shoddy performance. If you are going to do it at all you must do it well.'

She expressed herself quite pleased with the dress rehearsal, and said she thought they would not bring any discredit on themselves. Privately to Auntie she said:

'I think it's marvellous, what they have done in so short a time, but I don't want them to get puffed up about it.'

The day of the performance was a Saturday. Every available chair had been taken from the house into the barn, and some long benches had been borrowed from the farmer, Mr Martin. The invited visitors were the Rector, Jerry's father and mother, and three visitors from the house they were staying in, about a dozen neighbours, Mr and Mrs Martin from the farm, Mr Stidson, his wife, and three children, and various people from the village.

Auntie met the guests and showed them to their seats; Elizabeth provided them with programmes before going behind the scenes; Mummy was busy seeing to the costumes and make-up. Cook and the maids made themselves comfortable in their seats and prepared to enjoy themselves. At the last minute Mr Maclean, the boatman, turned up and said David had invited him.

At last all was ready. The audience was sitting prepared, most of them, to be very mildly amused, perhaps entertained, perhaps even bored.

A bell rang; the lights in the barn went out; the stage lights went up; the curtains parted to show the scene, and the play commenced.

CHAPTER V

Beginning of a Mystery

THERE was no question about the success of the play. The children received nothing but praise, and it was not the sort of praise that usually begins, 'Considering all things . . . '

There was no hitch in the working, no properties were forgotten, there were no mishaps, and no one dried up. Better still, each part was well spoken and every word was heard, not forgetting Elizabeth's 'invisible voices', heard off stage.

The play was about some children who cleverly outwitted a burglar, but the setting was designed to give scope for the wearing of some of the most exciting costumes from the big box. There was a ghost in it and a sliding panel, and the rescue of the heroine in the very moment of her despair. Some very noisy blank cartridges delighted the players and made the audience jump. Cook was heard to remark afterwards:

'Them blessed pistols made my blessed heart turn right over.'

After the final fall of the curtain, Mrs Mackie invited the whole audience to stay and do full justice to the refreshments she had provided. The boys described it as a 'feed', much to Jean's disgust. 'I hate people who "feed",' she said.

It was while they were all busy with the cakes and coffee, sandwiches and lemonade, that Jean's quick ears caught a half-whispered remark from Mr Stidson to a man he had brought with him.

'We shall have to get it done quickly,' he said. 'These children are all over the place, and they'll probably find out too much.'

Jean was terribly puzzled about this, especially as the two men separated quickly as soon as they saw she was looking at them. When she could get near Alan she tugged his sleeve.

'What is it?' he asked.

'Come outside a minute. I want to tell you something.'

51

'It can wait.'

'No, it can't.'

'It'll have to; I've got to help Mummy look after the visitors.'

'Just come out for a second,' Jean persisted. 'It's important.'

Alan looked sharply at her and saw that she wasn't fooling. 'All right,' he said, 'I'll come in a minute.'

As soon as he could he ran out to where Jean was impatiently waiting for him. She soon told him what she had heard.

'What could he be meaning?' he asked.

'I don't know, but there is something funny going on, I'm sure. D'you think we ought to tell Mummy?'

'Not yet. Don't let's tell anybody. As soon as we can get a chance we'll start doing some detective work.'

He paused, thinking for a few seconds. At last he said:

'I know. See if you can find David.'

'You're not going to tell him?'

'No, but he is sharp and can be useful. Find him and bring him out here a moment.'

In less than a minute Jean had dragged him from the feast, much to his annoyance.

'What do you want?' he demanded of Alan, rather crossly.

His brother thought a little flattery might smooth matters.

'Look here, David, old son,' he said. 'We want you to do something really important, and nobody in the house can do it as well as you.'

'What's that?'

'Keep your eye on Mr Stidson until he goes home. Don't let him think, or even suspect, that you are watching him. Try not to show yourself, but keep as near him as you can until he is safely on his way home. Take notice of the people he talks to; see if he tries wandering about our house anywhere; and ...'

'Is there something wrong?' interrupted David, his lost supper forgotten in the thrill of being called on to do detective work.

'We don't know, but we are suspicious. Just do what I tell you but don't breathe a word to a soul.'

'All right, I won't. I'll go and find him now.'

Immediately he hurried away.

'He'll do it,' said Alan. 'We must go in again or Mummy will wonder what's up. We'll decide what to do later.'

The children were allowed to stop up until all the guests had departed. Jerry and his people were the last to go, but as soon as the door was shut behind them, and their car could be heard running down the drive, Mrs Mackie said:

'The last item on this very delightful programme is BED. You have all done splendidly. Come and say "Good night", my dears.'

She started to kiss them all when she noticed that David was absent.

'Where *is* that boy?' she asked, with a sigh.

'Somewhere about,' said Auntie. 'I'll find him. Off you go, my dears.'

Before they had finished all their good nights they heard a loud commotion, and David came running in from the back to the accompaniment of loud cries from Edna.

'My word, you'll catch it. There's a state you're in. Don't carry all that mess in there.'

Mrs Mackie gave a little cry when she saw him. He was wet to the skin and water was running out and forming little pools all about him.

'What on earth . . . ?'

In spite of his condition David laughed.

'I fell in the stream,' he said.

'Fell in the stream! What were you doing near the stream at this time of night?'

'I just ran out a minute.'

'What for?' Mummy's voice sounded quite stern.

'I just wanted to go out for something a minute, and in the darkness I forgot about the stream and walked right into it.'

'What were you out there for?' demanded Mrs Mackie again.

Auntie interrupted. 'Let him get his wet things off and get into a hot bath.'

As soon as David was hauled off Alan hung back.

'Mummy,' he said, 'don't be angry with David. It was my fault, in a way.'

'How do you make that out?'

'May I leave it till the morning? We have a secret which we did not intend telling you . . . not yet . . . and David's accident has got something to do with it. Truly, Mummy, it is nothing wrong, only . . . '

'Well?'

'Only we may be wrong ourselves.'

'I'm afraid I don't understand you, but I shall want to know all about it in the morning.'

Alan kissed her lovingly. 'Thank you,' he said, 'for helping us so much and giving us such a jolly evening.'

Mummy smiled happily. 'I think you have all done so much to give us a treat that we ought to thank you.'

Alan did not get a chance of any further word with either David or Jean that night, but quite early in the morning the two of them assembled on Alan's bed. David was still laughing over his misadventure of the night before.

'I was following Mr Stidson,' he said, 'and it was dark. I saw him go and slipped out after him. He was hurrying and I soon lost sight of him. I ran to try to catch him up, and went plonk in the stream.'

'Yes, serves you right for being so stupid,' said Jean, 'but did you find out anything?'

'Nothing at all. From the time I left you I was near enough to him to hear all he said. He talked to the Rector about the crops and the harvest festival. He told Edna she was the prettiest girl he'd seen in these parts for years.'

'Oh!' cried Jean. 'It doesn't say much for the rest of them.'

'He only said that just to butter her up a bit,' said Alan. 'Go on.'

'He talked a bit to about a dozen people, but it was only just chat. He didn't go anywhere or do anything. In the end he went off in a hurry after looking at his watch. It seemed as though he had suddenly discovered he was late for something.'

'Didn't he go with his wife?'

'No, she went as soon as the play was over.'

'H'm,' said Alan. 'That doesn't help us very much.'

'No, but there was one rather funny thing,' added David.

'What was that?'

'Before he went he said something about having left his hat in the barn, and went that way, but he didn't go there at first. Instead he went down the passage until he came to the door of the room where you said you thought you saw a man that first morning.'

'Yes, yes,' said Jean, eagerly.

'When he got to the door, he turned round and saw me. Then he came back and said, "How silly of me. I've lost my way. I think I left my hat in the old barn." "Do you mean in our theatre?" I asked. "Yes, Sir," he said. "But we've always called it the old barn." '

'Well, what then?'

'There were lights still left on in the theatre, that's how it was he had spotted me. I went in there with him.'

'Did you find his hat?'

'It didn't take any finding; he was holding it in his hand all the time. When I told him he had it there he laughed and said, "I must be getting stupid." '

'Not so stupid as all that, I'm sure,' said Alan.

'What was he up to then?' asked David.

'We don't know, but you just keep quiet about it.'

'I'm sure he went to that room the first morning,' said Jean. 'I told you so at the time but you only laughed at me, and said he had gone up in smoke.'

'Very well,' said Alan. 'Promise not to say a word to anybody about it until I give you permission, and I'll tell you what we'll do.'

The promise was soon given and Alan continued:

'Get dressed quickly and quietly so that you don't disturb the others. I am going to have a look at that room, and you can come with me.'

'It is quite empty,' said David.

'I don't doubt it.'

'Do you think . . . ?'

Before he could finish his question he was cut short by Jean. 'We aren't too good at thinking; at least, that's what Auntie says; so we'll leave the thinking part of it and be up and doing. I'll be dressed in about two twinks.'

She dashed from the room, David following more slowly. Alan jumped from his bed and urged David out of the door with a good push from the flat of his foot.

In a very short space of time, so short that it did not speak very highly of the amount of washing they had done, they were assembled in the old part of the house. Michael and Elizabeth were both still sound asleep after their late and exciting night.

The first thing they did was to enter the room of mystery, as David called it. It was entirely empty as it was when they had visited it before, but this time they had come with the intention of examining it closely.

It was a square room, or almost square, about twenty-odd feet each way. The walls were of plain stone with no plaster or panelling. The reddish stone was bare and uncovered. The cement with which they had been built was still very good, and there was no sign of crumbling. The masonry was obviously of immense thickness, for the window, which was rather small for the size of the room, was set in a very deep recess, and had a sill or window-seat fully three feet from front to back.

'What does this window look out on to?' asked Jean, but before she could reach it, Alan, who had already been examining it, cried out, 'Stop!'

The other two looked at him curiously.

'Have a good look at this window-seat,' he said.

They all stared at it. At last Jean said 'Well?'

'This room,' said Alan, 'has obviously not been used for a long time, probably years. Look at the dust on the floor.'

'There are footprints; faint ones, but still footprints,' said David.

56

'Don't forget,' said Jean, 'that we all came in here and wandered round the other day.'

'Yes, I know,' replied Alan, 'but those aren't the ones I mean. There are several bits of mud round about this window.'

'So there are.'

'Yes, but that is not all. Don't you see that there is no dust worth speaking of on the window-seat?'

'I suppose that shows that somebody comes here and sits down to look out,' said David, 'and then takes all the dust away on the seat of his trousers.'

'Shouldn't be surprised,' said Jean.

'I should then,' continued Alan. 'Who would want to sit here to look out when all you can see from this window is that narrow bit of yard and a blank wall beyond?'

'What do you think then?'

'I hardly know yet.'

'Let the famous sleuth do his thinking undisturbed,' laughed David, 'and while he is thinking we'll do the work.'

'What work?' asked Jean.

'I don't know, but we'll do it.'

'Don't try to be funny, my lad,' said Alan. 'It doesn't suit you.'

As he said this Alan sat down on the window-seat and commenced, as he so often did, drumming with his fist and open fingers. It was a habit which had irritated Mrs Mackie so many times, but this time . . .

'Hi!' shouted David.

'What's up?'

'You and your everlasting tom-tom beating.'

'Go on,' replied Alan crossly, 'I'm not hurting you.' And he started drumming harder than before. Suddenly he stopped.

'Ah!' he cried. 'Do you notice what a good drum this makes? Listen.'

He started thumping and tapping again.

'It sounds very drummy,' said Jean. 'Quite hollow.'

David and Alan gave a shout together.

'Of course.'

'It *is* hollow.'

In a second they were both tugging at the wooden top of the window-seat. They pulled and heaved but could not shift it an inch. They spent a quarter of an hour struggling with it until they were all hot and dirty, but still it did not move.

'And yet I'm sure it is hollow underneath,' said Alan.

'I'll go and see if I can find some tools to hammer this woodwork to pieces with,' said David. 'Mummy won't mind. This room is never used.'

'Wait a bit,' replied Alan. 'I think we had better talk to Mummy about it first. We'll go now, it must be nearly time for breakfast. We can come back afterwards, and if we have her permission we shall not hesitate about chopping things about.'

'All right,' said Jean. 'I think that will be better. Come on. Shut the window, David.'

'It will be better to leave it open, I think. The place is so stuffy and musty,' answered Alan.

'You opened it,' said David. 'If you want it shut, then shut it.' As he said this he ran from the room.

'Cheeky brat,' said Alan, chasing after him, but Jean stopped a moment to close the window. As she did it she was surprised at the ease with which it moved on its hinge. She looked at it more closely and gave a little gasp of surprise as she saw that it had recently been oiled.

'Who can have done that?' she asked herself. 'Here's another mystery.'

She suddenly had an unaccountable feeling of fear and turned and rushed after her brothers.

At breakfast they told Mrs Mackie that they believed there was some secret passage leading out of that room, and asked her if they might do a tiny amount of damage in order to look for it. They carefully omitted to tell her anything about having twice seen Mr Stidson going to the room.

She smiled at their request. 'Do you think,' she asked, 'that you are going to find some hoard of gold or something?'

'We don't know,' said David, 'but we probably shall.'

'Well,' said Auntie, 'if you do . . . well, IF.'

There was a good deal of teasing, but the children were satisfied that Mummy was not going to interfere in their new exploit, so they went in search of tools as soon as they could. The two youngest children demanded to be allowed to join in the search, but as everybody had to stop to write their weekly letters to Mr Mackie before they were allowed to do anything else, it was some considerable time before they could start for the old part of the house again. David was the first away, and by the time the others arrived they found him doing a war-dance in the middle of the room.

'Clever me!' he cried. 'You are a smart lot of detectives bringing hammers and chisels and axes and things to hack a way into the secret treasure house, but I, I, myself, me . . . I, by my magic, have done the trick!'

'Trick? What trick?' they all cried.

With the air of a conjurer David told them to gather round.

'Now watch,' he cried. 'No deception, ladies and gentlemen. I have nothing up my sleeve. Just by my magic art I tap on the wooden top of the window-seat . . . like that . . . and with one finger I am able to lift up the seat which is hinged at the back.'

What followed was really laughable, for the children all eagerly reached forward to see him put his boasted magic into effect. He put his hand under the edge of the seat and tried to lift it, but it would not move.

'You fraud! What a sell!' were some of the cries which were hurled at David, but Jean noticed that he was not laughing at them.

'I tell you I did do it a minute ago,' he declared. 'I came in here and just for no reason that I can think of caught hold of the edge of this window-seat and it lifted up quite easily.'

'Tell that to Grannie's cat,' said Michael, rudely.

'It's true, I tell you,' blazed David, with an angry look in his eyes.

'Very well, do it again,' demanded Elizabeth, with a smile. 'If you can do it once you can do it again.'

David was almost ready to cry with annoyance.

'I can't do it now, and only two minutes ago it was as easy as can be.'

'Let's all heave together,' said Jean.

Heave they did, but to no purpose. At last Alan said, 'Look here, David, if that thing lifted up just now you can tell us what is inside.'

'No, I can't, except that I saw a deep hole. Just as I opened it I heard you all coming, so I let it drop quickly because I thought I would show you a bit of my pretended magic.'

'Come on then,' said Michael, 'another heave, all together.'

'Wait,' said Jean. 'Let's open the window first. I'm getting hot.'

She flung the window open and then clambered off the window-seat. 'Now let's try,' she said.

She set the example by taking a firm grip of the edge, and to her amazement and that of all the others the seat rose in her hand with practically no effort.

'There, what did I tell you?' said David.

'That's funny,' said Jean. 'It came quite easily.'

Alan was already peering inside. 'Look!' he cried, 'this goes down quite a long way. See, there is a wooden ladder you can just reach by hanging down from the top. I'm going down.'

'Carefully,' said Jean. 'It is dark, and the ladder may not be safe. We ought to have a torch.'

'There is one under my pillow in my bedroom,' said Micky. 'Shall I get it?'

'I will,' replied David. 'I won't be a sec.'

'Don't say a word to anybody,' Alan shouted after him.

He was soon back with the torch and they were able to examine their discovery. The lid which they had raised had a strong iron lock on the under side of it which obviously automatically fastened itself as soon as it was lowered into position. A short ladder reached to within a few feet of the top, and the light of the torch showed them that it was quite a good one.

'I should say it has recently been repaired,' said Jean.

They were all trembling with excitement as Alan lowered

himself into the hole and felt about with his feet for the top
of the ladder. Soon he was safely descending, shining a beam
from the torch in every direction.

'There is a tiny room down here,' he called. 'There is
nothing in it, though. Quite empty.'
'Has it got a door or way out of some kind?' called David.
'Can't see one.'

'I'm going down,' said Jean, and without any further word she flung herself over the edge and felt about for the ladder. In a few seconds she was beside Alan.

'No, nothing here,' she called.

'I want to come down,' shouted David.

'And I do,' cried Michael.

'And I do,' added Elizabeth.

'No, don't,' Alan called back to them. 'You might miss the ladder and have a nasty fall.'

'Rubbish!' said David. 'I'm not a baby.'

'You are not to come, I tell you.'

'You want to keep it all to yourself, I suppose, but don't forget I was the first to find the place.'

'There's nothing to come down for,' said Alan, from the bottom of the ladder, 'we are coming up in a minute.'

'All right,' said David, in a bit of a temper. 'Stay down there if you like.'

As he said it he pushed Michael and Elizabeth back and slammed the wooden seat back into its place again.

'Suppose you can't let them out now,' said Elizabeth.

'Serve 'em right. Why do they want to be so greedy?'

'They might suffocate down there,' said Michael.

'Not in a hurry they won't. I'll keep them down there a bit, and when they promise to let me come down too, I'll let them out.'

Elizabeth was looking anxious. 'You oughtn't to have done it, David,' she said. 'I'm going to let them out.'

'No,' cried David, trying to hold her back.

There was a bit of a struggle between them and while it was going on Michael snatched the opportunity to try to lift the lid.

'Now you have done it,' he shouted. 'They are trapped inside. The beastly thing is stuck again.'

David immediately left quarrelling with Elizabeth and tried himself to lift the seat. When he found it was quite immovable he was thoroughly scared.

'We opened it once, so we can do it again,' said Elizabeth, trying to comfort him.

'Twice you mean,' he said. 'But how it works I can't think.'

They struggled and pulled until they were in despair. Michael made matters worse by saying, 'I hope they won't be dead by the time we do get the thing open again.'

They were all nearly in tears when David said, 'Give me the axe. I'm going to chop a hole in the woodwork. That will give them air at any rate.'

'Wait a minute,' said Elizabeth, 'I've got an idea. I read in a story once about two boys who were trapped in a place and you couldn't open the door until some other door was shut.'

'But,' said Michael, 'this door has been open ever since we came in.'

'I know,' said Elizabeth, 'but the window hasn't.'

So saying she climbed up and pulled the window together and fastened it. Jumping down she said, 'Now try.'

They tried again, but still with no result.

'That's no good,' said David. 'Open it again.'

She did so, and as she did it she thought she heard a faint click. Without a word she stepped off her perch and once again put her hand to the wooden seat. With only the slightest effort she was able to raise it.

They shouted with delight at this success.

'You see,' she said, 'it has something to do with the window.'

They all shouted down to Alan and Jean, but received no reply. They kept on calling, but still there was no answer.

'They're trying to frighten us,' said David.

'I expect they are suffocated like I said,' insisted Michael.

After several minutes of calling and receiving no reply the children became really frightened and Elizabeth said, 'I am going to fetch Mummy or Auntie or somebody.'

'Wait just a minute,' said David. 'I have a few matches in my pocket left from those we took to the beach for our fire the other day. Help me to get down and I'll go and look for them.'

Soon he was on his way down the ladder. 'Don't shut me in,' he called.

'No fear,' said Michael.

The two at the top waited anxiously and watched him striking matches, but in less than three minutes he was climbing the ladder with all possible speed. When his head emerged he looked terribly scared.

'They're gone,' he cried. 'There is a little room down there without door or window and they are not in it.'

CHAPTER VI

The Priest's Hole

IT was a long time before Mrs Mackie could make any sense out of the tale the three very frightened children tearfully poured out to her, but she did not waste any time or words before following them to the scene of their misadventure. Auntie came, too, and they were both frankly amazed at what they were shown.

'You say they went down that ladder?' said Mrs Mackie.

'Yes.'

'Then they must be there now.'

'But they aren't.'

'My dear children, people don't dissolve; they went down, of that you're sure, consequently they are down there still.'

'I'm going down,' said Mummy. 'This torch of mine is a good one. They must be hiding in some dark corner, but I'll soon find them and then I'll give them beans for frightening you so.'

You notice that Mrs Mackie said 'frightening you'; she did not say 'me', although she was very thoroughly scared herself, but she had no intention of letting the children see it.

Without much difficulty she descended the ladder and the others all craned over to watch the beam of her torch as she drove it in every direction. They called to her, but for some while she did not answer. At last she called out:

'Let David come down a minute.'

David had been itching to go all the time, and at his mother's word he nearly fell down the hole in his eagerness to get there. When he arrived at the bottom he took a better look at the room which he already knew appeared to have no possible way in or out except the one he had come by. The floor was made of large slabs of stone firmly cemented in; the light of the big torch showed that plainly. The walls were smoothly plastered and were covered in paintings. David described it as 'sort of Christmas-cardy'. There were pictures of saints and the infant Jesus, scenes from Bible stories, all done in colours somewhat faded and rather crudely drawn.

Both Mrs Mackie and David searched the room foot by foot, but nowhere could they find even a mousehole, much less any place where the two eldest children could be hiding.

Mrs Mackie was more perplexed than alarmed.

'It stands to reason,' she said, 'the two children came down here, they didn't come up again, they aren't here now. There is only one possible solution.'

'What's that?' asked David.

'They have gone further.'

'But how?'

'It is our business to find out.'

'But there isn't a way out of here.'

'There must be.'

A call came down to them from Auntie. She was as anxious as the others to be doing something towards finding the missing children. It was hateful to have to stay at the top and do nothing except wait, so she cried down the hole:

'Can I do anything if I come down?'

'I don't think so,' answered Mrs Mackie, 'but come if you like. You may have an idea. I certainly have none.'

Auntie was down there almost before Mummy had finished speaking, calling back to Michael and Elizabeth:

'You stay there, and mind you don't fall. We don't want any cracked heads.'

Michael muttered something about the heads of all his brothers and sisters being cracked already, but everybody was too worried to take any notice. After Auntie, too, had disappeared into the gloom below he turned to Elizabeth and said:

'Let's have a lark with them.'

'How?'

'Let's shut them in.'

'No,' said Elizabeth. 'You might get them in there and not be able to get them out again.'

'But we know how to open it all right.'

'Don't do it, I tell you.'

'Dont be silly; it won't hurt; I only want to tease them a bit.'

'Yes, and perhaps suffocate them. You are not to do it, Michael.'

Elizabeth only called him Michael when she was cross with him; usually he was Micky or Mick to her. This time she was terrified at the thought of shutting anybody in the room below, and she was ready to do battle to prevent him from doing it.

'You know it was when David shut Alan and Jean in that they disappeared. Do you want Mummy to be lost, too?'

Michael had no intention of doing what followed. He took the lid of the seat in his hand and made as though he were going to let it fall into place. Actually, he was only trying to aggravate his sister, who was getting quite worked up about it. She, however, had no intention of running the risk of the same thing as had occurred before, so she made a grab at Michael to drag him away by force.

The result was a struggle, and down went the lid with a bang.

'There,' cried Michael, 'look what you have done!'

'It was you, you naughty boy,' declared Elizabeth.

'It wasn't; you did it through dragging at me.'

'You shouldn't have touched it.'

'I never meant to close it.'

'Well, open it, and don't be so silly any more.'

Michael put his hand to the window-seat and again found it would not move.

'Silly,' said Elizabeth. 'Don't forget the window. You've got to move the window backwards and forwards before you can unlock this.'

In a few seconds they were once more peering down the hole.

'Are you all right?' they called.

There was no answer.

Again they shouted; louder this time, a dreadful fear adding power to their lungs.

Still silence.

'Oh!' cried Elizabeth. 'What shall we do? You naughty boy; it is all your fault; now they've gone, too.'

Michael was very silent. He was ready to cry, but managed to hold back his tears.

'What are we going to do?' demanded Elizabeth again.

'Let's shout again.'

'Shouting is no good.'

'No, it isn't,' came a laughing voice from below them. David's head appeared out of the darkness.

'I frightened you,' he said, as he scrambled out of the hole.

'Where are Mummy and Auntie?' asked Elizabeth, with much relief in her voice.

'Gone,' said David, still laughing.

'Tell us what has happened,' pleaded Michael.

'Well, I don't know exactly, but while we were there searching the place for an opening, suddenly a part of the wall moved back. It was really a door, but it had been painted so cunningly as part of a picture on the wall that we had not spotted that it was a door.'

'How did you open it?'

'We didn't. It just opened itself; I don't know how.'

'I believe I know,' said Elizabeth. 'You remember I found out that you could only open this thing after the window had been opened and shut again.'

'Yes.'

'Well, I told you I had read something of the sort in a story. It was about some boys who explored a monkey temple in India in one of the old forts.'

'I know that one; I've read it,' said David.

'Well, I expect that the door in the room below only opens when the seat cover is closed down.'

'Ah!' cried David. 'You did close it, didn't you? I thought I heard it bang down.'

'Yes, Micky wanted to close it and I didn't want him to, and between us we let it fall.'

'What a lucky thing!' said David. 'It showed us just what we wanted to know; how to get out of that room into the passage beyond.'

'Is there a passage?'

'Of course there is, stupid.'

'All right, you need not be so free with your stupids,' said Michael. 'You did not tell us there was a passage.'

'Well, there is. You see, when the door mysteriously opened I was the first to see it. I called to Mummy and we all three went inside.'

'Did you see Alan and Jean?' interrupted Elizabeth.

'No, but we all started to hurry down this passage. It was very dark and we could not see the end of it, and it was sloping downwards all the time. We had not gone far when Mummy stopped and made me come back to make sure the door did not close behind us. Just as I got into the room again the door did shut, and then I heard you calling, so I thought I would have a bit of fun by not answering you.'

There was a pause for a minute, and then Elizabeth said: 'But are Mummy and Auntie safe? And are they able to get back?'

'Well,' replied David. 'I hardly know. They are certainly shut in somewhere along the passage.'

'But can they get out?'

'I don't suppose they can,' replied Elizabeth, 'unless we close down this seat again and wait to hear them call from below.'

'I'll tell you what I'll do,' said David. 'I am not afraid of being shut in. I'll go down again and you can imprison me. By doing that the door in the wall will be open, and I can watch for their return.'

'There is no need to do that,' said Michael. 'We can shut this lid down again and the door will open. When they come back they will shout for us to let them out, won't they?'

'I suppose so. All right,' agreed David. 'I will stay here with you and wait for them to come back.'

The truth is that David had no wish to be shut in a dark hole all by himself, even though he knew he could get out whenever he called to the others. He would have done it had it been necessary, but he was quite glad there was no need for him to do so.

They sat down to wait as patiently as they could. As usual,

David had all sorts of things in his pockets, and he was able to fish out a very dirty and crumpled pack of cards, so they tried to pass away the time by playing a game of 'Fish'. They had played one game through and were about to start another, when there was a sound which attracted their attention. Somebody was in the corridor outside the room. They could hear footsteps.

They listened very intently, but the sound had stopped. David got up and tip-toed across to the door. He was just about to peep out when, with a loud whoop, Alan and Jean dashed in.

'How on earth did you get out there?' asked David.

'Where on earth have you been?' demanded Michael.

'What on earth have you been doing?' queried Elizabeth.

'One at a time,' said Alan, still laughing.

Still the questions poured out.

'Where are Mummy and Auntie?'

'How did you get out of that hole?'

'Have you found any treasure?'

'How many secret rooms are there?'

'Did you meet anybody?'

'Were you very frightened?'

'Tell us all about it.'

'Give us a chance,' said Jean, 'and we will.'

'What are you saying about Mummy and Auntie?' asked Alan. 'We haven't seen them.'

'They went down there to look for you and went down a long passage and haven't come back.'

'Listen, and I'll tell you all about it.'

'I've been down,' interrupted David, 'and seen the door in the wall open and the long passage and all that.'

'Have you?' said Alan. 'Well then, there is no need for me to tell you anything.'

'Yes, there is. I only went just inside because Mummy sent me back.'

'Well, when we were down there, for a long time we could not find any door or way out except the ladder we had climbed down. Then suddenly a door in the wall seemed to open by itself.'

'Yes,' interrupted David again. 'That was when I shut the seat down.'

'We guessed that. At once we went through the doorway so strangely opened and started to walk on. After a while we came to some steps which seemed to be cut out of rock, and we did not know whether to go any further or not. We decided to come back and tell you what we had found, and then go on again.'

'Yes,' said Jean, 'and then when we did return we found we could not open the door. We were trapped.'

'We weren't really,' said Alan, 'but we thought we were, which was just as bad. After a few tears from Jean . . . '

'Rubbish!' cried Jean. 'I didn't cry. Besides, it was too dark for you to see.'

'You sniffed a lot, anyway,' continued Alan. 'If you like it better I'll say after a few sniffs from Jean we determined to follow the passage as far as we could. We hurried down the steps and found that the rocky tunnel then turned sharp to the right. Ahead we could see a faint speck of light, and we could certainly smell fresher air.'

'I think I know now,' said David.

'Are you telling this tale or am I?'

'Go on.'

'It was only about five minutes after that when we found ourselves in a cave which opened out on the cliff just above that place where all the masses of rock and boulders are piled up at the end of our beach. It is almost impossible to see the cave entrance from below, but there is a fairly easy way to climb down. As soon as we were down we raced along the beach and ran home to let everybody know we were safe.'

'H'm,' said Michael. 'I said we should have adventures down here.'

'Alan and I have had the adventure,' said Jean. 'I don't see where you come in.'

'Now you have found the smugglers' cave and the secret

passage,' said Michael. 'I'm certainly going to have my share in all the adventures. You see if I won't.'

Michael did not know how true a word he was speaking.

'Didn't you find anything there worth finding?' asked Elizabeth.

'Not a thing,' replied Jean.

'We did not really stop to look very carefully,' said Alan. 'We were rather anxious to make sure we could get out safely. You say Mummy and Auntie have gone down to look for us?'

'Yes.'

'They'll be safe enough. It is not a dangerous climb down from the cave. Let us go and meet them.'

At that all the children went off in a body and made all possible speed to the beach. They were about half-way along when they saw Mrs Mackie and Auntie coming towards them. They gave a loud cheer and ran to meet them. They were, of course, overjoyed to find Alan and Jean none the worse for their exploit, and eagerly compared notes with them.

'What's the time, Mummy, please?' asked Elizabeth.

'Almost twelve, dear.'

'Is that all?' said Jean, in a very surprised tone. 'I thought it was much later.'

'Why? Are you hungry?'

'No, Mummy, only it seems hours and hours since we first climbed down the ladder into the little secret room, and yet it is only about an hour and a quarter.'

'I know,' said Auntie. 'We seemed to be ages crawling along that tunnel.'

'Crawling?' cried Michael. 'Did you have to go on your hands and knees?'

'No, Micky, but we could not hurry. There was only just room to get through, and I was afraid of putting my foot into a hole all the time. I didn't want to turn my ankle over.'

As they wandered along the beach Mummy signalled to Alan to drop back with her a bit. Auntie saw the signal and set the other children to the task of looking out for a certain kind of shell she wanted.

'You want me?' said Alan, taking her arm.

'Yes, my son. Did you see anybody about the cave or on the rocks as you came through?'

'Not a soul.'

'Quite sure?'

'Quite. Why?'

'Well, both Auntie and I thought we heard voices, men's voices, just before we entered the cave; in fact, we held back a bit before showing ourselves.'

'Yes?'

'We did not see anybody, so walked out boldly. Then we were quite sure somebody had been there, for there was a strong smell of tobacco.'

'Like a strong, shaggy sort of pipe tobacco?'

'Yes.'

'Ah!' said Alan.

Mrs Mackie waited for him to say more. At last she asked, 'Why do you say Ah! like that?'

'Have you ever noticed the smell of Mr Stidson's pipe?'

'No, he never smokes while I am talking to him. Why do you ask that?'

Then Alan told his mother all they knew about having seen Mr Stidson using the secret passage. When he had finished Mrs Mackie said:

'I wonder what he can be doing that for. You had better keep a watch on him. There may be nothing wrong, but I can't see why he should want to do that. There is no reason why he should ever go into the old part of our house. One thing is certain, somebody smoking a smelly sort of pipe had been in the cave between your leaving it and our entering it.'

'I think,' said Alan, after a pause, 'that cave will want exploring.'

The seven of them arrived home feeling healthily hungry. As they trooped across the garden Mrs Mackie asked:

'Who is that man going across the back of the house near the barn?'

The answer came in a chorus, 'Mr Stidson.'

CHAPTER VII

Lost

THE next few days passed comparatively uneventfully. On the Sunday the whole Mackie household went to the tiny church, where they sat in the Oxmouth Manor pews, which had not been occupied for a long time. On Monday and all the week the weather was gloriously fine; they all bathed and boated, rode and fished, played cricket, took photographs, filled every minute of each wonderful day. Yet all the time they were all thinking of one thing, the further exploration of the secret room and passage.

The next wet day was the signal for an almost unanimous remark at breakfast time.

'Mummy . . . '

They all stopped and looked at one another.

'Mummy . . . '

Each looked around waiting for one of the others to speak what was in every mind.

'Yes, dears, a very suitable day for it,' said Mrs Mackie.

They all pretended to be very dense and not to know what she meant. But she smiled at them all and continued:

'When I hear that particular tone of voice I know that there is some special request coming, and as it is a very wet morning obviously you want to do something indoors. I am as curious as you are about the places we only half explored the other day and, as I said, this is just the day for it.'

'Hurrah for the jolly old pieces of eight!' cried Michael.

'If you find anything, my lad,' said Alan, 'it will probably be a few pieces of plate, or rather, plates. If there ever was any treasure there you can bet your best shoes it has gone to the melting pot long ago.'

'May we all come down into the hole?' asked Elizabeth.

'Yes,' replied Mummy, 'I think it is quite safe. We'll help you down the ladder.'

'Is Auntie coming, too?' inquired Micky.

'No,' said Auntie, 'I don't think I had better come: I have got rather a lot to do. The weather has been so lovely that I have left undone several jobs that I ought to have done.'

'And there is no health in us,' whispered David.

'Perhaps it is just as well,' said Michael.

'Why?'

'Well, you see, Auntie, if we went and got ourselves shut in there you would be the only one to know where we were and able to get us out.'

'A bit of safety first,' said Jean.

'How many torches can we muster?' asked Alan. 'We shall want plenty of light.'

'I have a good acetylene cycle lamp which I have held ready for the purpose,' said Mummy. 'It will give a brilliant light and will burn a long time. We can take torches as well, as a stand-by in case the other fizzles out.'

By the time all the preliminary arrangements were made and they were ready to descend the ladder the children were almost wild with impatience. As soon as the window-seat was lifted Mummy looked round and said, 'Are we all here?'

'No, David has disappeared somewhere,' said Elizabeth in a tone of disgust. 'He would be the one to keep us waiting.'

'Just run and bring him along, Alan,' said Mrs Mackie. 'Tell him if he can't come at once we shall not wait for him.'

Alan dashed off and came back in a surprisingly short space of time, declaring he could not find him anywhere. He had asked Auntie and she said she had seen him start off with them, or at any rate, that is what she thought.

Mummy was annoyed at his absence and did not want to go without him, but the other children were clamouring to make a start.

'It's his own fault,' said Jean. 'He knew we were starting, and if he can't come he must do the other thing.'

'Very well, then,' said Mummy. 'Alan go first, and then Elizabeth and Michael. Help them down, my son, and then

Jean can go. I am coming last so that I can shut the trap down on top of us. Unless I do that we shall not be able to get into the rocky passage.'

The children, especially the younger ones, were trembling with excitement as Mummy shut them into the tiny dark room, but soon she was beside them and had turned up the flame of her lamp so that they could see every detail. Elizabeth held rather tight to Mummy's hand and said:

'Oo! Isn't it creepy?'

'No,' said Jean. 'There's nothing creepy about it.'

'It's all very well to say that,' retorted Micky, 'when there is a bright light here, but I shouldn't like to be shut in if it was dark.'

'Is this a kind of priest's hole?' asked Alan.

'I expect so,' replied Mrs Mackie.

'What a stuffy sort of place to have to live in. Fancy hiding in a place like this, perhaps for weeks at a stretch.'

'Yes,' added Elizabeth, 'and always the danger of being discovered.'

'I think the greatest danger was the chance of dying of starvation,' said Mummy.

'Why?'

'Well, suppose someone was down here hiding when the house was occupied by enemies. It might be almost impossible for anyone to smuggle food down to him.'

'I read a story once,' said Alan, 'about an old house like ours where they discovered a priest's hole and the skeleton of a long dead priest in it.'

'No horrors, please,' said Mummy, fearing that the younger ones might be made nervous, but, used as she was to Michael's unexpected remarks, she was not prepared for what followed.

'I wish we could find a skeleton,' he said. 'Wouldn't it be jolly.'

'What an idea!' cried Mrs Mackie. 'I shouldn't think it would be at all jolly. But come on, we must not waste time. I'll lead with my big lamp; Alan can come last.'

In single file they started down the passage.

'We're a band of smugglers,' said Michael. 'We are just going down to bring in a cargo. I wish I had a sword.'

'Why a sword?' asked Jean.

'Pirates always wore swords and used them if there was a scrap.'

'Thought you were talking about smugglers,' said Alan.

'Same sort of animal,' replied Jean. 'Picturesque on the stage or in story books, but most unpleasant persons to meet in real life.'

They went steadily on, silent for a while, until Micky spoke again:

'Pity David isn't here.'

'It's his own fault that he isn't.'

'I know, but I wish he had come, all the same.'

At last Mrs Mackie turned the lamp down very dim. 'Look ahead,' she said.

They all looked and saw a small but bright point of light in front of and below them.

'Is that the cave?' they asked.

'Yes, it is still a long way off and you must go very carefully for the rocks are slippery, and I don't want a twisted ankle.'

At last they reached the fresh air of the cave, and all had a feeling of relief. After a time Alan said:

'We haven't made any fresh discoveries. The tunnel does not seem to have any other passages opening out of it. We had better explore the cave now and see if it has any more openings.'

As he spoke he started to look well about him. There was a heap of fallen rock at one side of the cave and he made for that. Just as he was about to clamber over to see behind it there was a loud screech and he jumped back, looking decidedly scared.

'What was that?' demanded Mrs Mackie.

'I don't know,' said Alan. 'Something dark jumped up at me and made a horrid noise.'

'Let's go back again,' said Elizabeth.

'We ought to have brought Chris,' said Jean.

'We haven't even got a stick between us,' said Mummy. 'I wonder what it can be.'

They all stood huddled together for a moment or two, and then Alan advanced again. Once more he climbed over the broken rocky pieces, but very slowly and with one eye on a sudden and undignified retreat. Mummy gave him her support by coming fairly close behind him. The others kept very much in the background.

This time he saw nothing and moved over the top.

'Nothing here now,' he called, but as he spoke there was a louder shriek than before, and in the hollowness of the cave it sounded dreadful.

Alan jumped yards and nearly knocked his mother over in doing so.

'Do let's go,' said Elizabeth. 'I think this is a beastly place. Come, Mummy, do.'

'Yes,' added Micky. 'It's haunted.'

'Rubbish!' said Mummy. 'I want to hear that noise again. All of you keep quiet a minute.'

'I don't want to hear it any more,' said Elizabeth.

'Nothing to be frightened of, sweetheart. You listen with me. We'll solve the mystery pretty soon, unless I am mistaken.'

They all remained breathlessly quiet, but no further sound came. Mummy signalled to Alan to go gently forward again. He was a bit nervous, but he put a bold face on it and started to climb once again. He had hardly moved three yards, however, when there came shriek after shriek of uncontrolled laughter. The cave rang and echoed with it. Mummy and the children looked at one another and with one voice cried, 'DAVID!'

In a couple of seconds he came scrambling from his hiding-place.

'What a fright I gave you,' he laughed. 'Didn't Alan jump! And even Mummy was scared.'

'I think you are a rotten practical joker,' said Jean.

'Come here,' said Mummy. 'How did you manage to get down here before us?'

'I wanted to play a trick on you.'
'That is not answering my question.'
'I just ran; that's all.'

'But how did you manage to get down the hole before us?'
'I didn't.'
'Then how . . . ?'

'I just raced down to the beach, climbed the rocks into this cave, and hid and waited for you.'

'You must have got very wet.'

'No I didn't. I wore my raincoat.'

'Where is it?'

'I was so hot with running that I took it off. It is over there where I was hiding.'

While this questioning was going on Alan was nosing around. Just behind the heap of fragments of rock which had hidden David he found that the cave ran back and up into a narrow point. His torch did not show him very much, and he was just scrambling back to the others when Mrs Mackie called out to him.

'Alan, just look and see if David's raincoat is there and bring it along.'

'I can't see it,' he called.

'I threw it down in there somewhere,' shouted David.

'Bring me Mummy's lamp,' Alan replied.

Jean struggled over the ragged rocks with the lamp, and Alan turned the screw round to give a full blaze of light. He soon spotted David's coat, lying just where he had thrown it in his eagerness, but before he stooped to pick it up the beam from the lamp showed him something that made him pause. At the extreme end of the narrowing part of the cave was a black patch, just where the floor rose to the roof.

'What are you looking at, Alan?' asked Jean.

'Nothing,' he said, turning the beam of light away. 'Take that coat back; I'll be with you in a second.'

'You can't turn me off like that, you know,' said Jean. 'Tell me what attracted your attention? You spotted something, I know you did.'

'I don't think it's anything.'

'Point the light round that way again; then we'll see.'

Reluctantly again Alan drove the beam of light towards the dark patch, and they both saw at once what he had suspected, that there was a hole there, leading to some further cave.

'Can't we keep this to ourselves?' said Alan. 'At any rate until we have had a chance of exploring it.'

'All right,' replied Jean. 'Mum's the word!'

They clambered back to the others and were greeted with many questions as to why they had been so long.

'We were only taking a good look round,' said Jean.

'I don't think you had better go to that part of the cave too much,' said Mrs Mackie. 'The roof doesn't look at all safe to me. I shouldn't like to see one of you with a cracked head.'

Elizabeth, ever practical, asked, 'Well, what are we going to do now?'

'Go back the way we came, I suppose,' said Mrs Mackie. 'The rain is still pouring down and we shall get very wet if we go down to the beach. It is obvious that there is no other hiding-place than the one we came through, and the rocky tunnel has no more openings. I'm sorry to disappoint you, Micky, but I'm afraid your dream of treasure is only a dream.'

'Anyway,' said David, 'it's jolly to know that we have a real genuine priest's hole in our own house.'

'And a secret passage,' said Michael.

'And a smuggler's cave,' added Elizabeth.

In a few minutes they were all once more in procession up the tunnel. Mrs Mackie put David close to her this time to make sure that he did not go off on some other mad stunt of his own. Presently they came to the end, and to the astonishment of all of them the passage was blocked and they could not get into the priest's hole.

'We left this door open, didn't we?' said Mrs Mackie.

They were all quite sure that no attempt had been made to close it.

'Must have swung to,' said Alan.

'Doubtful,' replied Jean.

'I can't find any way of opening it,' said Mummy. 'It seems to fit solid into the rock. Unless we had come through such a short time ago I should have said there was no possible way into the room.'

'Just the same on the other side,' said Alan. 'Until the

door opened by itself it was impossible to tell that there was any door there.'

'Hey!' suddenly shouted David. 'Look here. Here is something.'

'What is it?' asked Mrs Mackie.

'A narrow opening here at the side. I wonder what's in here.'

They turned all the lights in that direction and saw that there was indeed a very narrow opening in the wall of the tunnel, just about large enough for a man to squeeze through.

'I wonder why we did not see that when we came down,' said Jean.

'For a very obvious reason,' replied her mother. 'When the door was open it masked this hole and we could not possibly see it. It is only now that the door is shut that there is a way in.'

'Let's go and see what is in there,' cried Micky. 'Lead on with the light, Alan.'

'Shall I, Mummy?' asked Alan.

Mrs Mackie was frowning and thinking hard.

'Stop!' she said. 'This door can only have been shut . . . Ah! Look out!'

Hastily she leapt back, dragging the foremost children with her and knocking over the others in her haste. As it was she was only just quick enough, for the great heavy door which had so effectively barred their way swung back in their faces.

When they had recovered from the confusion and had picked themselves up they pressed forward into the priest's hole. David at once started to climb the ladder.

'Oh!' he called. 'We can't get out. It's impossible to open this trap from the inside.'

'How stupid of us not to think of it,' said Alan.

'I am the one to blame,' said Mummy. 'But I still can't think why that door was closed and then opened of its own accord.'

'I think I know,' said Elizabeth. 'Somebody must have been coming down. When the trap in the window-seat is open the door into the tunnel is shut, isn't it. It was when we shut it that the door opened.'

'Of course,' said Jean. 'But who can have been coming down?'

'Perhaps it was Auntie,' said Micky. 'She may have been looking for us.'

'That must be it,' said Mummy cheerfully. 'Let's all stand at the bottom of the ladder and shout. If it was Auntie she can't be far away and she will hear us.'

They all coo-ee'd and shouted until they were almost deafened by the echoes, but there was no reply from above. After about ten minutes of this exhausting exercise Mummy said:

'It is a dreadful nuisance, but we shall have to go right back into the cave again and then along the beach.'

'And shan't we get wet,' said Jean.

'That can't be helped.'

'I know, Mummy,' said Alan. 'Let me run down the tunnel and back by the beach. It won't take me long. It is better for me to get wet than for all of you. I'm not afraid of a drop of rain.'

'Let David go,' said Jean. 'He has his coat; besides, he came that way for the pleasure of trying to frighten us; let him have the pleasure of making a long journey for the honour of letting us out.'

'Go yourself,' said David.

'No,' said Mrs Mackie. 'I think it will be a just punishment for you, my lad. You go, and you are to hurry. I'll time you. See how quick you can be. We'll sit down here and tell stories until you liberate us. Come on, you can be the rescue party, to relieve the imprisoned explorers.'

Put that way, David couldn't make any more excuses for not going. They gave him a torch and set him off down the tunnel.

'I hope he won't come to any harm,' said Mummy, almost as soon as he had started.

'He's all right,' said Alan. 'He has plenty of sense and pluck when he likes to use them. He won't be very long. You'll see.'

In a remarkably short space of time, as it seemed, they heard a sound above them, and a beam of daylight showed them that the trap had been lifted. The children began to scramble up the ladder, eager to get out of the dark and stuffy hole.

'Alan, hold on to Elizabeth,' called Mrs Mackie. 'Alan! Where are you?'

Suddenly Jean began to laugh. 'The great silly,' she said, 'he has gone and got himself shut in the tunnel again. He was nosing about all the while you were telling us that story and of course when David lifted the flap he was trapped.'

'Now, what are we to do?' asked Mummy.

'Well, we must go up, shut the flap, and so let him out. Then we can open the flap again and up he comes.'

'Very well, then, up you go.'

Soon they were in the blessed daylight once more. At once they shut down the window-seat, opened and shut the window to release the catch and then opened the flap again. They called to Alan, but there was no answer. They kept on calling, but still no reply.

'Now, what's gone wrong?' said Mrs Mackie wearily.

'Let me go down again and see' said David. 'You must shut me in for a minute or two, so that I can look for him in the tunnel.'

Without waiting for permission he slid down the ladder. From the bottom he called to them to shut him in.

'Wait three minutes and then open again,' he called.

What a long time three minutes did seem. At last Mrs Mackie said, 'Now open.'

They opened and found David waiting on the ladder.

'Well?' they all asked.

'Nowhere down there,' he said. 'I went right into the tunnel and called, but he simply is not there.'

CHAPTER VIII

Michael's Adventure

'I AM beginning to wish,' said Mrs Mackie, when they were once more back in the dining-room and sitting down to lunch, 'that I had less inquisitive children. These disappearances are getting monotonous. First Alan and Jean can't be found, then David is lost, and now Alan is missing once again.'

'He'll be all right,' said Auntie, to set her mind at rest, although she was a bit unsettled herself.

'I dare say he will, but it is worrying. I never feel too happy about wandering in caves. My worst dreams as a child were always connected with being hopelessly imprisoned in some underground tunnel.'

'Alan can take care of himself,' said David. 'He came all the way back from Switzerland by himself, didn't he?'

'If he doesn't come soon,' said Micky, 'I will search for him.'

'And get lost yourself,' said Jean.

'No I wouldn't.'

'You might.'

'It wouldn't matter. We can do without him,' teased Elizabeth. 'Three boys in a family is too many.'

'Yes, three too many,' said Jean.

'Smile, Mummy,' cried Micky. 'There is nothing to worry about. I'll find him.'

Mrs Mackie could not resist the infection of Micky's cheerfulness, and she laughed aloud.

'Splendid!' she cried. 'As long as I have stout fellows like you to stand by me I shall be extremely lucky.'

After lunch there was still no sign of Alan, and even the other children began to look glum. They could not keep any conversation going on any other subject, even though they manfully tried. At last Auntie spoke.

'I know what is the best thing to do. Elizabeth, Michael, and David can have a quiet afternoon with their books. You had better lie on your beds and rest. While you are doing it, Mummy, Jean, and I will start a new search for him.'

There was a chorus of cries of protest at this suggestion, but Jean's voice was powerful enough to drown the opposition, and she used it so effectively that Mrs Mackie had to tell her that she would be the one compelled to rest on the bed if she didn't make less noise.

With many grumbles at being deprived of further exploration, the 'three kids', as Jean rudely called them, were shooed off with their books and magazines, and within a very few minutes the whole house was very quiet. Mummy, Auntie, and Jean had departed, there was no sound from the kitchen quarters, and nothing was to be heard except the ponderous ticking of the pompous clock in the hall. In fact it was so quiet that Michael looked across at David's bed and was astonished to discover that he had fallen asleep almost immediately.

At once Michael's mind began to roam through those regions of imagination which were so real to him in the magic time of lying in bed waiting for sleep. Within a few minutes his lips were moving, and he appeared to be in most earnest conversation with someone.

These imaginary conversations of his were a daily occurrence, and once Mrs Mackie had overheard one of them. She had asked him:

'Who were you having a chat with, old son?'

Very solemnly, without any trace of shyness, and in the most natural manner, he had replied:

'Only my friend.'

'And who is your friend?' Mummy had asked.

'Peter.'

'Peter who?'

'No, Peter nobody; just Peter.'

'But who is he?'

'Just my friend.'

'Where does he live?'

'Oh! here, of course. He always lives where I live. He told me he couldn't possibly live anywhere else.'

'What is he like?'

'Rather like me, I should think, except that he's very small.'

'I wish I could see your friend Peter,' said Mrs Mackie.

'I don't think you ever will,' Michael had replied. 'You see he's shy. The minute he thinks anybody might see him, except me, he hides at once.'

'Where is he hiding now?'

'Ah!' laughed Michael. 'That's telling, isn't it, Peter?' Then, after a pause, he added: 'He says he thinks you are rather nice, but he is not going to be caught.'

On one occasion Micky had been asked how he knew a certain thing. His answer was: 'Peter told me.' His cousin Peter happened to be present at the time and answered rather hotly:

'I'm sure I never told you anything of the sort.'

'Not you, MY Peter,' said Michael.

The other children had started a good deal of teasing about that, and wanted to know who his Peter might be, but Mrs Mackie had cut them short, for she understood that to Micky his little unseen friend was very, very real.

Now, on this afternoon, when the house was so quiet, he was holding a whispered conversation with Peter. It went on for some time, and then he nodded his head several times and said aloud: 'All right. We'll both go.'

Quietly he slipped off the bed, silently he crept down the stairs, like a mouse he opened the front door and peeped out. To his relief the rain had stopped, so he tip-toed out until he thought himself safe from any pursuit by Nora. Then he ran fast to the farm, never heeding the puddles and mud.

Presently it was a very splashed and red-faced Michael who knocked at the door of the farm kitchen. Mrs Martin opened the door and started hastily wiping her hands on her apron when she saw who it was.

'Well, young gentleman,' she cried, in her jolly voice, 'what can I do for you?'

'Please,' said Michael, 'I wanted to see Mr Stidson.'

'Oh! did you? Want the pony or something? He's about somewhere, I saw him pass the window a minute ago.'

'No, it's not the pony, thank you, but I wanted to speak to Mr Stidson. It's rather important.'

'Can't you give me a message?'

'No, I'm afraid I can't. You see, it is something rather private.'

Mrs Martin laughed. 'Oh! a secret; I see. Well, just you come in a minute and have a piece of my cake while I send the boy to look for him.'

'Thank you,' said Michael, 'but I'm afraid I can't stop to eat anything now. Can I come tomorrow?'

'Yes, my dear,' she replied, looking curiously at his very anxious expression. Then, in a loud voice, she cried:

'Tom! Just run and find Sam a minute. Tell him one of the young gentleman wants him particular.'

In a few minutes Sam Stidson appeared. He looked very surprised when he saw Michael and his tone was not too pleasant when he asked him what he wanted.

'Can you come out in the road with me for a few minutes?'

'Whatever for?'

'Something tremendously important,' said Michael.

Growling something about being late with the milking the man followed him just outside the farm gate.

'Now then, what is it?' he demanded.

'My eldest brother is lost,' said Micky, going straight to the point.

'Lost is he?'

'Yes, and I want you to go with me to find him.'

'But where is he lost?'

'Down in the priest's hole, or in the rocky tunnel, or in the smugglers' cave; anyway he's down there somewhere.'

'But I don't know what you mean. Priest's hole?'

'Oh! yes, you do know,' said Michael very boldly, although he was feeling rather quivery inside.

'I tell you . . . ' began Stidson again.

Michael cut him short with a remark which mystified the

man. 'You see, my friend, Peter, he has just told me to come to you.'

'Peter? Who's Peter?'

'No one you know, but he told me you could help us find Alan because you know all about those secret places. I know that's true, too, because we have seen you going there.'

There was a pause for several seconds, in which Sam looked distinctly hot and bothered.

'Come on,' persisted Michael. 'I don't want to have to bother Mummy with what Peter told me, but I shall if you don't help me quickly.'

'Where is your mother now?'

'Down there, looking for him, with Auntie and Jean.'

There was another pause, and then the man seemed to make up his mind. 'I'll come across and see your mother this evening,' he said.

'No, that won't do,' said Micky. 'Alan may be in great danger . . .'

'No, he won't come to any harm,' interrupted Sam.

'How do you know?' asked Michael.

'He can't. He's safe enough down there.'

'I dare say he is, but I want to be the one to find him, and I simply can't do it by myself, so I have come to ask you to help me.'

'But I can't get away till the milking's done.'

At that moment Mr Martin came out to the gate and called 'Sam!' Then catching sight of Michael, he grinned and said: 'Hullo! young man. When are you going to give us some more of your plays? I enjoyed the last one. Have you come over to ride or something?'

'No,' said Michael boldly, 'but I want you to do me a favour.'

'Certainly, if I can. What is it?'

'I want you to let Mr Stidson off his milking this afternoon. I want him to help me . . . and it's very urgent.'

'And my cows being milked is urgent, too.' Then, turning to Sam the farmer added: 'What's up?'

'One of the children lost.'

'Eh? Then why ever didn't you say so at first? Of course you must go. I'll get Missus to help with the milking for once. 'Twon't be the first time. Where is he lost, sonny?'

Michael was very much tempted to reply that if he could answer that question Alan wouldn't be lost at all, but he was just able to hold his tongue, shaking his head vigorously.

'Get along, then, Sam, and if you want more help you must let me know, and I'll organize a party from the village.'

'I'll find him all right,' said Sam, starting off with Micky trotting at his side.

As soon as they were out of Mr Martin's hearing Sam said: 'Let me hear all about it.'

Michael then told him all that had taken place that morning, finishing up by saying:

'The more I thought about it the more sure I was that you were the person to help. Then my friend told me to come to you, too, and I always do what he tells me because he . . . '

Mr Stidson interrupted. 'Wait, I've just thought of something. You mother doesn't know you are here with me?'

'No, nobody knows except Mr Martin.'

'Ah! he knows, of course. But have you thought what a fright your mother will be in if she gets back and then can't find you?'

'Coo!' said Micky, his favourite expression of surprise, 'I never thought of that. She would have what Alan calls gustus verticalis.'

'What on earth is gustus . . . what you said?'

'Oh, that's Latin. He learns Latin at school, and it means "wind up". But really, it's a bit awkward. What are we going to do?'

'The best thing,' said Sam, 'will be to let me go and look for him while you go home and wait till your mother returns.'

'No, I can't do that. I promised Peter I would go, and this is going to be my adventure.'

'Then you are going to let your mother get worried to a fit?'

'My Mummy never gets fits. If she is worried she gets two straight lines between her eyes and that's all. Perhaps she feels all funny inside, but she doesn't go all potty. I'm sorry about it, but we must risk it.'

Mr Stidson stood still in the road. 'Look here, sonny,' he said, 'I shall get on much quicker and better if I go by myself, so you just run off home and leave the searching to me.'

Very stubbornly Michael stood his ground. 'No,' he insisted, 'I tell you I am coming too.'

The man was getting impatient, when there was a sudden doggy rush round the corner, and Chris was bounding and jumping around them, his tail wagging from side to side so fast that it was just a blur.

'Aha!' cried Micky. 'Here is our messenger. Come here, Chris.'

'What are you going to do?'

'Wait a second and you'll see.'

From his pocket Michael produced a very much worn dilapidated diary which he had faithfully carried for over a year and a half. He tore out one of the few clean pages and with a very stumpy pencil he wrote on it:

'I am going with Mr Stidson to look for Alan. Michael. P.S., My Friend, P., you know, is coming too.'

He folded this over and on the outside he wrote, 'Mummy. Strikly private from Mick.'

He drew from his pocket a thoroughly black piece of frayed string and tied the note securely to Chris's collar, and then sent him scampering home.

'There now,' he said, 'that will be right. Mummy will see my note and not worry about me. Now we can go on.'

Rather sulkily Mr Stidson started forward again.

'Where are we going?' demanded Michael.

'If you wait long enough you will see.'

The man strode on and took no further notice of the little boy trotting along beside him until they came to a very rickety gate that led into a tangled and overgrown wood.

'Mind you don't get your legs scratched,' he said. 'It's rough going here.'

'All right,' replied Michael. 'Where does this lead to?'

'If you wait long enough you'll see.'

'You said that before. Why are you cross?'

There was only a grunt in reply, and they pushed on in silence again. Micky's legs were bleeding in twenty places from the rough clawings of the brambles and his shoes were full of water and mud, but he paid no heed to any of these discomforts. He seemed to be talking softly to himself and was saying something about 'rescue party'.

Presently they came to a ruined cottage in a moderately clear space in the wood. It had no roof and the windows were merely gaping holes. Charred rafters were sprawling in grotesque and tipsy attitudes inside, while weeds grew man-high right up to the door. With white paint somebody had smeared across the only bit of sound wall remaining the name, 'Spion Kop'. . . .

'What a funny name,' said Michael.

'Funny place, too,' said Stidson. 'I got a bullet in the shoulder there.'

'What, here?'

'No, South Africa. Come on, we can't stop to talk about the Boer War.'

He led the way round behind the ruined house, and to Michael's intense surprise at the back there was a little stone hut which was in a very good state of repair. From his pocket Stidson produced a key and opened the door.

'What place is this?' asked Micky.

'If you wait long enough you'll see.'

'If I were you,' said Michael, 'I would have a gramophone record made of that remark; it would save you such a lot of trouble.'

'Would it? Well, it'll save you a lot of trouble if you just go inside and stop talking.'

'In here? But Alan isn't here, is he?'

'No, but you are,' said the man, pushing him inside so roughly that he fell over.

Before Michael could get to his feet again, or recover from the surprise of this sudden action on the part of Stidson, the door was slammed on him and he heard the key turn in the lock.

It was not quite dark in there, and he quickly made a dash for the door and tugged at it with all his strength shouting at the top of his voice:

'Let me out! Let me out! Mr Stidson, let me out!'

He hammered and kicked at the door, he hurt his toes and hands, and his voice broke with the effort of his yelling, but the result was nothing. The door would not budge, and there was no reply to his calling. At the end of a minute he knew that he was trapped and a prisoner.

He was only a little boy, and he became very frightened. He sat down on the floor and cried until he was quite worn out. Then, when the first terror was over he began to think sensibly, and before long he was carrying on a conversation in a quiet voice.

'Are you there, Peter?'

He answered himself. 'Yes, I'm here.'

'Why did you tell me to go to Mr Stidson? You ought to have known he was going to do something like this.'

'I didn't know, but it will be all right.'

'How do you know?'

'Mr Martin will ask him where you are. You have sent a note by Chris to Mummy, so she will know.'

'But suppose I have to stay here all night?'

'You'll be quite safe. I shall stay with you.'

'I wonder when they will start to look for me.'

'Soon.'

'Why has Mr Stidson shut me up like this?'

'I don't know, but if you wait long enough you'll see.'

'Did he tell you to say that?'

'No, but he said it so many times that I think it must be true.'

'I'm hungry.'

'Pity you didn't have Mrs Martin's cake when she offered it to you!'

'Yes. I wish I had it now. Oh! I remember, I've still got a piece of chocolate in my pocket from yesterday. Have a bit?'

'No thanks, you eat it.'

Silently Micky ate his piece of squashy chocolate, and either that or his conversation with his imaginary friend did good, for he stood up and made an examination of his prison.

It was a square stone cell with the front wall about eight feet high, and a rough roof sloping to the back wall which was a couple of feet lower. The light came from a tiny window at the top of the front wall, too high for Michael to reach, and too small for him to squeeze through even if he could have done so. There was absolutely nothing in the hut in the way of furnishing or even rubbish. The floor was made of flat slabs of stone.

Presently Micky began to feel cold, for he had been thoroughly wetted in pushing through the wood, so he started to jump about to warm himself. As he did so he felt one of the slabs of stone wobbling under his feet. He stooped to look at it, and found it was quite loose. After a hard struggle and several broken finger-nails he was able to raise one end of it enough to get a grip of it. Then he heaved with all his might and managed to turn it over on to one side. To his great astonishment there was a hole below it in which was a wooden box. The light was now getting so dim that he could not see very well, but he felt sure the box was either the one they had seen in the wreck or another exactly like it.

He tried to lift it out, but it was too heavy for him. The excitement of this new discovery drove his fears from his mind, until at last it became quite dark and from sheer weariness he lay down on the hard floor again.

For a few minutes he held a whispered conversation with Peter again, and then there was silence.

Michael was asleep.

CHAPTER IX

Spion Kop

WHILE these strange misadventures were befalling Michael, Mummy, Auntie, and Jean found Alan quite simply. What had happened to him was this. He had been curious to examine the small passage which they had discovered opening out behind the door which led from the priest's hole into the rocky tunnel. He had slipped into the tunnel to wait for the closing of the door so that he might get into the little passage which they had seen but had not investigated.

As soon as he saw the door shut he squeezed himself through the narrow opening. His torch showed him that it led into a small cave which smelt very musty and stuffy. He strode boldly into it and stabbed the darkness with the beam of his torch in all directions. The first thing he noticed was that the dusty floor had evidently been trampled over a great deal. Then, in one place, he saw where someone's pipe had been knocked out. In another spot he found a cigarette end.

'Someone has been here quite recently,' he said to himself. 'I wonder who that can have been. Stidson, I shouldn't be surprised. Well, he didn't come here for nothing, so I'll see if I can't find out what he did come for.'

Foot by foot he cast his light about examining every part of the ground. Then he searched the walls and roof, and was just about to admit reluctantly that there was nothing there when something whitish in appearance caught his eye. Eagerly he ran forward and found that a hollow place had been scooped out of the rocky wall at the ground level and a box had been pushed inside.

Trembling with excitement he pulled the box out and was very surprised to find that it was a twin brother to the one they had seen in the wreck. The wood felt wet, as though it had been submerged in the sea for some time.

'Now I'm going to solve the mystery,' he muttered. 'Hope the beastly thing isn't locked.'

It was just at that time that David had gone down to look for him, but he was so intent on what he was doing that he did not hear his brother's calls.

To his annoyance the box was locked, and his fingers were not strong enough to wrench it open. Still, he was not going to let himself be beaten easily, and he gave a tremendous kick just under the fastening. Nothing gave, so he kicked again. This time he hurt his toe, so he became more cautious until at last something snapped and the lid flew open.

In a second he was on his knees peering into the box. He found it was zinc-lined with a pneumatic cover which fitted very close so as to make it water-tight, but his disappointment was intense when he found the wretched thing was empty.

He now began to feel the atmosphere very close and oppressive, so he closed the lid of the box and pushed it back into its niche. Then he wriggled his way through the passage again.

'Must be a tight squeeze for Stidson and Co., whoever the Co. may be, to get through here,' he thought. 'He's not a very big man but he is pretty bulky. I should think he dragged a few buttons off coming through here.'

At this moment he was suddenly confounded by realizing that he was shut in. He heaved himself against the door which had opened back on him, but although he made it quiver he could not move it an inch.

'What a silly ass I am,' he said. 'I ought to have known what would happen. Oh, well! I need not worry. They will come down to look for me, and as soon as the window-seat is lifted this door will move back into place. Then I shall be able to get into the tunnel. I hope they won't be very long for I am almost suffocating already.'

With his torch he examined the door which was holding him prisoner, but he could see no hope of moving it. At the bottom it did not fit very close to the floor of his rocky prison, and by lying down he could feel a faint breath of fresher air.

After some while he became bored with doing nothing, and

not a little nervous at the long delay in his liberation. He found himself getting scared. It was intensely dark, for he would not risk the failure of his torch by keeping it burning all the time. At last he could stand the waiting no more, so he went back into the cave again and hauled out the box once again. He asked himself why was the box locked if there was nothing in it. The thought set him to work examining it again.

This time it did not take him long to discover that the box was at least three inches deeper on the outside than it was on the inside.

'The wood can't be as thick as all that,' he told himself. 'There must be a hollow space in the bottom.'

After several minutes of tapping and pulling and pushing at the sides and bottom of the box he found that he could lift the zinc lining right out. It came out quite smoothly and easily, and, sure enough, there was something underneath the bottom of it.

'Hullo! What's here?' he cried aloud.

Laid carefully in a bed of cotton-wool were six wide glass tubes. Each was carefully sealed at both ends. Alan picked up one of them and examined it. At first he thought it was empty, but a little bubble of air moving inside showed him that the tube contained a coloured liquid.

'What on earth can this be?' he asked himself. 'I'll take one of these away with me and put the rest back.'

In his excitement he almost dropped the glass tube as he thrust the inner lining of the box into place, closed the lid, and pushed the whole back into the hollow from which he had taken it.

By this time he was in a fearful state of heat and semi-suffocation, and he made once more for the door. To his immense relief he reached it just as it began to move.

'Somebody coming down. Thank goodness, now I can get out and have some fresh air; yes, and some grub, too.'

Suddenly a new thought struck him. 'Suppose it isn't one of my own people but Stidson or, perhaps, some other man.'

He did not feel very comfortable, but scrambled out into

the tunnel, taking great breaths of the purer air. He ran a little way down in case he might have to hurry away from some undesirable visitor, but he was soon relieved to hear his name called.

How vigorously he replied! 'Righto! I'm here. I'm coming.'

Mrs Mackie, Auntie, and Jean were rejoiced at finding him so quickly, and wanted to know what had happened to him. He explained to them where he had been, told them about his discovery, and showed the glass tube.

At this Mummy surprised him very much by saying:

'Well, before anything else is done that tube must be put back again.'

'Why?'

'I don't want them, whoever they are, to know that the secret has been discovered.'

'But I broke the lock.'

'Yes, that's a pity, but they need not know that you have found the secret of the tubes. No, it must be put back. Auntie and Jean can go up and work the door for us to get in there, and they can let us out again in about five minutes' time.'

So it was arranged and so it was carried out. Alan and Mrs Mackie went back into the little cave and restored the tube to its place, and presently were safely back in their house once more. They arrived exactly one minute after Michael had sneaked away. It was not until tea-time that they missed him, for they thought he was still on his bed, reading or sleeping.

When it was discovered that he was not in the house the first thought of everyone was that he had taken advantage of the lull in the rain and had gone down to the beach. Alan said he was none the worse for his adventure, so he would go down to fetch him. Within half an hour he was back saying there was no sign of him.

Now there was real consternation. Mrs Mackie was really upset this time.

'I wasn't so worried about Alan, but Micky, after all, is only a very little boy, and is even young for his age,' she said.

'He's got heaps of sense,' replied Auntie, who was always his champion. 'He won't come to any harm.'

'But suppose he is lost down there in those beastly tunnels and caves.'

'How can he be? We have just come from there, and he certainly did not come down.'

'Unless he went along the beach.'

Chris at that moment came in and flopped himself down at Mrs Mackie's feet, looking up with such a pleased expression that she was bound to take notice of him.

'Hullo! Chris, you dear old thing,' she said. 'I wish you could put us on his track. Where's Micky, eh? Where is he? Did you go somewhere with him?'

Chris's answer was to put his paws on her lap and wag his little tail like mad. Mrs Mackie put her hand to his neck to pat him when she suddenly looked at him very sharply.

'Whatever have you got on your collar?' she cried.

In two seconds she was reading Michael's note.

'Splendid Chris!' said Alan.

'Sensible Michael!' said Auntie.

'If he is with Mr Stidson he will be all right,' said Mrs Mackie.

'I wonder!' added Alan.

'You don't doubt it, do you?'

'I don't know, Mummy. There is something queer about him. I'm going over to the farm to see if they know what has happened.'

'I'll come with you,' said Auntie.

'Let us all go,' said Mummy. 'The walk after this wet and trying day will do us good.'

After tea they all went to the farm and saw Mr and Mrs Martin, who told them of Mick's visit and departure with the man Stidson.

'Mighty mysterious about it he was, too,' said the farmer. 'Nice little chap! He seemed very determined.'

'I shouldn't worry, Ma'am,' added Mrs Martin. 'He isn't likely to come to any harm with Stidson.'

'Are you sure of that?' asked Alan.

'Well, I . . .'

'Yes?'

'Well, I suppose so. Stidson's a steady chap, and he has been with us for five years.'

'Is there still any smuggling done in this part of the coast?' asked Auntie.

'Plenty of it, Miss. It's easier today than it was in the old times.'

'Easier?'

'Yes, I know there are plenty of fast boats for chasing them and all that, but modern smuggling is done with racing motor boats. The old-fashioned chain of pack-horses with their loads of brandy and silk and tobacco and such-like no longer exists, but speedy motor cars take their place. Why, only about five years ago there was a gang broken up at Barwithy, a bit farther down the coast.'

'What had they been smuggling?' cried Jean, who was quite thrilled at the turn the conversation had taken.

'All sorts of things, Miss. Anything that there is a heavy duty on pays for smuggling; high-priced wines, for instance. But I'm told one of the things they smuggled was that sugar stuff . . . what's it called? . . . I remember reading about it . . . it's supposed to be about seven hundred times sweeter than sugar.'

'My word!' cried David. 'I'd like some of that.'

'I don't think you would, my son, you simply could not bear the taste of it.'

'What is the stuff, Mummy?' asked Elizabeth.

'Saccharine, I expect, but I think I've read about some other chemical like it that is even sweeter.'

'But it wouldn't pay people to smuggle only that, would it?' asked Auntie. 'I shouldn't think there was enough of it wanted.'

'A smuggler, Miss,' said Mr Martin, 'is like a poacher. If he has got it in his blood he must do it. Why, I knew a doctor round here years ago who was quite well off and one of the best liked men in the county.'

'Good reason for why,' interrupted Mrs Martin. 'He'd do

anybody a good turn, and he'd take more trouble to look after a poor chap who couldn't possibly pay him than he would over his rich patients. I've seen him leave a cricket match three times during the game to go and look at an old feller who was almost dying.'

'But, as I was saying,' went on the farmer, 'this old doctor was a born poacher, and nothing would cure him of it. It was

just the excitement of bagging something that didn't belong to him, right under the noses of the keepers. That was the whole point, right under the noses of the keepers.'

'It was the adventure of it, I suppose,' said Alan.

'Yes, my boy, it wanted a daring man to do it, and he was daring, if you like. Oh! I could tell you some tales about him.'

Mrs Martin began to laugh.

'I should think so. One of the best bits about him I remember was this. We had a whist drive down at Oxmouth in aid of something or other and the old doctor gave a brace of pheasants as first prize for ladies. Well, I won it. I had wonderful cards that night, and I didn't strike any terrible partners, for a wonder. Anyhow, I won these pheasants, and as I went up to receive my prize the old doctor burst out into a roar of laughter.

' "What's the joke?" I said.

'And in front of all that room full of people he bellowed out, "Oh! they're only going home again." He had pinched those pheasants off our land. Shameless he was, shameless!'

'Yes,' added the farmer, 'and if he hadn't been trained for a doctor he was just the sort who would have been a poacher and smuggler for the pure enjoyment of running risks.'

'But all this talk about smugglers and poachers has got nothing to do with finding your little boy, Ma'am,' he said.

'I don't know so much,' said Alan. 'We know a bit more about your man Stidson than you seem to know yourself.'

'Eh? What's that?'

They told the farmer all they knew after he had promised not to repeat what he heard. He was frankly amazed when he heard that there was indeed a secret passage leading from the Manor House to the shore.

'Although, mind, there have been tales about such things. I never took much notice of them because they say the same of all old houses.'

'But Stidson would never do any harm to a little boy, I'm sure of that,' said Mrs Martin.

'No, he has always behaved quite nicely to the children when he has taken them out riding,' said Mrs Mackie.

'No, I shouldn't worry, if I were you. I can't think where he can have taken the child to be away so long, but they'll come to no harm. I expect the boy will be home again by the time you get back.'

'I'm sure I hope so,' said Mummy. 'Thank you, Mr Martin.'

'If he doesn't come soon let me know, Ma'am, and, of course, if I can help in any way you must send over for me.'

The family departed for home, after Mrs Martin had given them all some fine new apples, just picked. On their way they met Jerry, who had not been to see them for two or three days.

They had to tell him all the adventures that had befallen them, and he made Mrs Mackie smile by solemnly suggesting that they should try to get bloodhounds to search for Micky.

'I don't think it has quite come to that yet,' said Auntie.

'Wouldn't it be thrilling, though,' said Jean. 'We should see headlines in the papers, "Bloodhounds search for lost boy." '

'Shut up!' cried Alan. 'You'll be making Mummy nervous in a minute.'

As soon as they reached home Mummy suggested that they should all go to the beach for a swim.

'There is just time,' she said.

As a matter of fact she wanted to give all of them something to do to keep their minds busy. She had an uncomfortable feeling about Michael that she could not shake off, and she could see that the others were getting on edge, too.

A good struggle with the breakers did them all good, and they came back from their bathe feeling invigorated and less anxious. Still, when they arrived at the house, and darkness was falling and there was yet no sign of the missing boy, their anxiety came on with increased force.

'I'll wait just another half hour,' said Mummy, 'and then, if he isn't here I shall ring up the police. Come on now, it is past bedtime for David and Elizabeth.'

'Oh! Mummy,' they both cried.

'You can't do any good by stopping up, my dears.'

'No, but it is useless thinking about sleep.'

'You are better in bed,' said Auntie, shepherding them off to their rooms.

'It's not fair,' protested David.

'Make Alan and Jean go, too,' demanded Elizabeth.

In spite of all protests they were soon in bed, and contrary to their own declared intention of stopping awake, they were both asleep in a very short while. They were not so worried about Micky as the grown-ups, and it would have taken more than that to keep them awake after the invigorating tussle they had had with the great waves.

Mrs Mackie could hardly keep her eyes from the clock.

'Five more minutes,' she said, at last, but at the same moment they were all terribly startled by a loud crash at the dining-room window, followed by the sound of falling broken glass.

'Whatever's that?' they cried with one voice, and after a pause there was a rush to see what had happened.

'Someone has hurled a brick through the window,' said Alan.

'Then where is the brick?' demanded Jerry, who was nosing about among the broken glass. 'Hullo! what's this?' he cried.

'What is it? What is it?' eagerly asked Mummy and Auntie.

'Why! A great big key. Look, it has a piece of paper tied to it.'

Mrs Mackie snatched it from him and took it over to the light. Scrawled on the piece of paper were two words:

'SPION KOP.'

'What on earth can that mean?' cried Mummy.

'What key is it?'

'What does SPION KOP mean?'

'Why was it thrown in here?'

'Who can have thrown it?'

'Is it meant to be a message or something?'

Everybody was asking questions, but nobody waited for any answer. They were all completely mystified.

At the first crash of the broken window Chris had started barking furiously and had run out through the kitchen into the back, where they could hear him growling savagely.

'Hark at Chris,' said Alan. 'Come on, Jerry, we'll see if anyone is there.'

They dashed out, grabbing at a couple of golf clubs as they went. They ran round to the back of the house where the dog was still making a fuss, but they could find nobody. Cook had come out, armed with a huge ladle, prepared to do battle with some spirit.

'My blessed senses!' she cried. 'If I can get at the blessed varmints that done that I'll give 'em a crack on the blessed head with this blessed thing. Blest if I won't.'

She had to return to her kitchen disappointed, for there was no one on whom she could expend her wrath.

'No one there, Mummy,' said Alan, coming back disappointed at not having a chance to hack at an intruder with his iron club.

Mrs Mackie was still puzzling over the words on the scrap of paper. 'What have I heard about SPION KOP?' she said.

'It is the name of a battle-place in both South Africa wars,' said Auntie. 'I can remember the second one. It happened when I was a girl.'

'It doesn't tell us anything, does it?' queried Mummy. 'What had we better do? I think it is definitely a case for the police now.'

They all agreed, and just as Mrs Mackie was about to pick up the phone there was a loud peal at the front door-bell. They all looked at one another.

Alan snatched up his golf club again. 'Come, Jerry!' he cried. 'Round the back, quick! Mummy, don't have the door opened until Jerry and I can get behind whoever it is.'

Before Mrs Mackie could warn him not to attack any unsuspecting and innocent person he was off. The ring at the bell was followed by a loud hammering at the knocker. Mrs Mackie opened the door herself, Auntie standing close beside her.

'Good evening, ma'am.'

Jean burst out laughing; she really couldn't help it.

'Oh! Mr Martin,' said Mummy. 'You gave us quite a fright.'

'Sorry, ma'am, but I can't rest. Stidson hasn't come back, and I wondered if you had heard anything about the young gentleman.'

'Come in,' invited Mummy. 'I'm really thankful you have come. We have just had a mysterious happening. This was thrown through our window.'

The farmer just glanced at it.

'SPION KOP,' he shouted. 'Come on, I know what that means.'

'What does it mean?' asked Auntie.

'It's where we are going to find your little boy.'

'But Spion Kop's in South Africa,' said Jean.

'Don't I know it,' he answered. 'But not this Spion Kop. We gave it the name for a lark. I know where it is. The two boys and you, ma'am, had better come with me. We shall want lanterns.'

'Can we take our golf clubs?' asked Alan, still disappointed at having been cheated out of using them.

'Yes, they'll be useful for knocking down brambles.'

'Only brambles!' cried Alan. 'Isn't there a chance of a scrap?'

'If I thought so I shouldn't take you and your mother. Come on!'

CHAPTER X

Elizabeth Makes a Capture

ALAN and Jerry had one of the biggest thrills of their young lives making this journey through the wood at night, hacking a way through brambly patches, splashing across boggy places, helping Mummy over the worst obstacles.

'Rescue party smashing a trail through the jungle to rescue of kidnapped white man,' said Alan.

'Mr Martin is Trader Horn,' replied Jerry.

'And what am I supposed to be?' asked Mummy.

'You are merely the mother of the prisoner.'

'Thank you. "Merely" did you say?'

'No, you are the brave Englishwoman who accompanied the rescue party to show that jungle rescues from savage tribes is no longer only a job for men.'

'That sounds a little more complimentary.'

So they went on talking cheerfully while they struggled against the obstacles which were constantly tripping them up.

'I haven't been here for years,' said the farmer, 'and this wood has not been thinned out for a long time.'

'Do you think you can find the place?' asked Mrs Mackie anxiously.

'Oh! I'll find it all right, but it may take a little while. Why, here it is!' he cried.

The ruins of the old burnt-out house looked ghostly in the light of their lamps.

'Surely nobody lives here,' said Alan.

'No, an old couple did live here a good many years ago, and they refused to move, although Squire offered them a better place. Then, on Saturday night, while they were in the village doing their bit of shopping, the place caught fire, and before they got back there was nothing left but what you see. They were so upset at having to leave it that they were both dead within a month.'

All the while he was talking Mr Martin was scrambling about among the ruins. At last he said:

'I can't see any place where anybody can lie hid. There isn't a door standing anywhere in the place, so I can't think what the key is for.'

Suddenly Alan startled them all by saying in a very excited whisper, 'Listen!'

'What is it?'

'Listen, I say!'

They all stood quite still and switched off their torches and listened intently. There were sounds of somebody or something moving through the wood. The sounds came nearer and nearer. Alan slipped his hand into Mummy's and Jerry crept close to them both. Mr Martin whispered to Alan:

'Let me have your golf club. If I fetch somebody a crack with that he'll not want another.'

For a few seconds there was complete silence. Then the sounds of movement started again, accompanied by a little whimpering noise. Mummy startled them all by a loud cry:

'It's Chris. Our dear old Chris; he has come to find us.'

'Yes, and perhaps to find Micky, too.'

'If he is here anywhere,' said Jerry, 'hadn't we better shout. If he hears us he will answer.'

'Unless he is gagged,' said Alan.

Mummy shuddered. 'Don't!' she said.

Chris came bounding through when he heard their voices, his tail wagging as though it would come right off. He jumped and ran round them in circles.

Mr Martin spoke. 'Perhaps you are right, my boy; let us all shout together and then listen carefully.'

'I'll count three,' said Mummy, 'and then all call together, a long drawn-out note. Now then, one, two, three.'

'Mi-i-i-i-i-chael,' they called.

Echoes and then silence. Again they called. Two labourers who had just entered the wood to set some wires for rabbits heard the noise and saw the flashing of the torches dimly through the trees, and bolted for their lives. They made straight for the 'Masons' Arms', where they revived their sagging spirits with a long drink. As soon as they could do so they told the assembled company that the wood was haunted. They were laughed at, but they persisted in their story and declared they had seen the ghosts and heard them.

The story soon spread and increased with each successive telling, until it reached the ears of the boatman, Maclean.

'Eh?' he cried sharply to the man who told him, and then without waiting for an answer made off for the Spion Kop wood. He ran until he reached the edge of the wood and then he went more cautiously. Hearing sounds of approaching people he crouched down in a bed of wet bracken and watched.

Soon he saw the dim figures of a man with a little boy on his back, followed by a woman very closely; after them came two boys and a dog. As they passed he heard the boy on the man's back say:

'It was really Chris who found me, wasn't it, Mummy?'

'Yes, my dear.'

'I've had the biggest adventure, haven't I, Mummy?'

'Yes, and it was almost too big.'

'I don't think so; I wasn't really very frightened; at least, not for long.'

They passed out of Maclean's hearing, and he muttered to himself:

'Kidnapping, eh? This is something new. What can they have done that for? There is work for me to do.'

Swiftly and silently he sped back to Oxmouth. Within five minutes of entering the village he was out of it again on a bicycle making for the larger village of Sidford, about six miles farther inland. He stopped there at a public telephone box, and was in there quite a long time. At last his business was done and he cycled slowly back to Oxmouth.

Meanwhile Micky had been borne home in triumph. He was greeted like a conquering hero. Cook called him her blessed lamb until he stopped her by saying she usually cooked her blessed lamb in the blessed oven.

He had to tell over again the story of what had happened to him. When he had finished Mummy took up the tale.

'Yes,' she said, 'after we had shouted ourselves hoarse he had not heard us, he was so sound asleep. Chris found him and barked to us to follow.'

'H'm,' said Martin. 'That shed has been repaired and had a door and lock put on it since I was there last. I'm amazed about that fellow Stidson. I'm going down to see the bobby at Oxmouth, not that he's much good, but I'm going to set him to work to see if the man is still anywhere about. Good night everybody, I don't think you will have any more trouble tonight.'

'Thank you, Mr Martin, for all you have done.'

'Only too pleased, ma'am. Hope the little boy will be none the worse.'

Jerry went with Mr Martin because Mrs Mackie did not like him going home alone, and it was getting very late.

'Please, Jerry,' she said, 'will you make me a promise.'

'Certainly I will.'

'Don't say a word to anybody about what has happened here tonight. We don't want to be the centre of a nine-days' wonder. We should be having some inquisitive reporters around here in no time.'

'Right, I'll be mum. Good-bye.'

In a minute they were gone, and soon the Mackie household had settled down to rest. Before she went to bed Mrs Mackie went in to satisfy herself that Micky really was asleep in his bed, and then she took Chris in and laid him at the boy's feet.

'Sleep there, Chris,' she whispered, 'and bark like mad if any intruders come.'

The night was quiet and peaceful, and when morning came no one was any the worse for the mishaps of the previous day. Michael remarked what was in everybody's mind, that it did not seem as though yesterday's events were real. Quite early, Mr Martin came round to inquire for Michael, and seemed very surprised to find him looking so well and jolly.

'No sign of that man of mine,' he said, 'and I don't expect there will be. He's off for good, I expect, but what's behind it

I cannot imagine. Makes me short-handed, too, just as I am cutting corn. I wonder if the young people would care to come round this afternoon. I expect to finish off the first field if nothing goes wrong, and there should be heaps of rabbits.'

'Thank you, Mr Martin,' said Mrs Mackie, 'perhaps we will bring our tea and picnic out there. What field will you be in?'

'The one we call thirteen acres. It's just beyond the second stile on the footpath from our farm to Sidforth.'

'Hooray!' cried Michael; 'perhaps I shall catch a bunny and bring it home to keep it for a pet.'

'Yes, and perhaps you won't,' said Jean.

Mr Martin had barely left when they had another visitor. Maclean, the boatman, called.

'Don't you think it is too rough for boating today?' asked Mrs Mackie.

'Yes, ma'am, much too rough. I didn't really come about that. I wanted to speak to you privately, if I might.'

'Certainly. Come into this room, will you?'

Mrs Mackie led the way into her little workshop, as she called it. As soon as she had closed the door, she said:

'What is it you want?'

'I would be glad if you would tell me exactly what happened to your little boy yesterday.'

'What do you know about it?'

'Very little, and I want to know more.'

'Might I ask why?'

'Because I am trying to collect evidence against certain people down around here who are guilty of law-breaking in the matter of smuggling.'

'I know nothing about smuggling.'

'Of course you don't, ma'am, but you can tell me about your little boy being shut up in Spion Kop.'

'Who told you he was shut up there?'

'He did.'

'But that's impossible.'

'Forgive me, madam, for being so stupid. I always begin a

story at the wrong end. I only know about your son being kidnapped because I heard him say when Mr Martin was carrying him through the wood, "It was Chris that found me, wasn't it?"'

'What were you doing in the wood?'

'Being inquisitive.'

'Well, don't you think you might mind your own business about this matter?'

'I'm sorry, I didn't mean to appear rude. It really is my business. I have been living in Oxmouth for two and a half years for the express purpose of laying by the heels a very clever gang of smugglers.'

'What do they smuggle?'

'Anything on which they can make a profit. They send out the proceeds of various robberies, and they bring into the country anything on which a heavy duty may be avoided.'

'You must excuse me, Maclean,' said Mrs Mackie, 'but I do not feel this has anything to do with me, and I have a great deal to do this morning.'

'I regret taking up your time, ma'am, but if you would only tell me just what happened yesterday it might be a great help to me.'

'And I regret that I cannot say anything. The little misadventure that befell my son is happily ended with no ill effects. I wish the matter dropped, and I shall be extremely grateful to you if you will remain silent on the subject.'

Still the man persisted.

'Will you tell me one thing? Had the man Stidson anything to do with it?'

Mrs Mackie walked to the door and opened it, and he walked out without another word. When he reached the hall he turned and with a pleasant smile to the children he said:

'I think we might take some spinners and try for mackerel as soon as the sea gets quiet again; that is, if your mother will allow you to come.'

There was a loud chorus of 'Oh! do, Mummy. I'd just love to go mackerel fishing. Do let us, Mummy.'

'We'll see,' replied Mrs Mackie, and then a thought seemed to strike her, and she followed Maclean outside. 'One minute,' she said. 'Is that suggestion about the fishing a hint to me that you'll get from the children what I refuse to tell you?'

'The thought had not entered my mind, ma'am.'

'It would be a waste of time trying to pump them, I assure you, for if my children want to keep a secret nothing will drag it out of them, nothing.'

'Ah! so there is a secret.'

The man departed laughing to himself and Mrs Mackie re-entered the house frowning. She could not be sure whether she had done the right thing in choking Maclean off as she did.

Of course all the children wanted to know what he had been so secret about, but Mummy was not inclined to be any more communicative to them than she had been to him. This was one of the occasions when she missed Daddy very much. She would have liked to feel that he was at hand to help in a problem that was worrying her.

However, she would not let the children see her looking glum, so she set everybody to work on various jobs, and then went with them to the beach for a bathe. On the way down somebody said something about the wreck again, and Michael suddenly exclaimed:

'Oh! you know that box we saw in the wreck; well, there was one just like it in the hut where I was imprisoned.'

'Don't you mean incarcerated?' teased Alan.

'No, I mean what I say.'

'I didn't see any box there when we fetched you out,' said Mummy.

'No, nor I,' added Alan.

'Well, there was one there, any way. It was hidden in a hole in the floor under one of the slabs of stone. I tried to lift it out but it was too heavy.'

'Was it just like the one in the wreck?' asked Alan.

'Exactly, I think; as far as I can remember.'

'Curiouser and curiouser,' said Mummy.

'What is? And why is it?' asked David, but he did not wait for an answer. He had seen a bird that was strange to him on a bush near the edge of the cliff, and he was crawling along to get a near view of it.

While the children were bathing, Mrs Mackie told Auntie all the details of her interview with Maclean, and asked her if she thought she had done right in refusing to give him any information.

'I don't know what to think,' replied Auntie. 'Of course he is obviously not a man of these parts. Perhaps what he said was quite true.'

'Yes, but I don't want this affair to be magnified in the children's minds. If Michael lets his brains run on thinking over and over about his kidnapping he will begin to get nervous and that I want to avoid.'

'I think he has almost forgotten about it already. It certainly is not worrying him.'

'You heard what he said just now about the hidden box. That shows he has not forgotten.'

'No, not forgotten exactly, but it is not in the front of his thoughts.'

'Of course he was not kidnapped in the ordinary sense of the word. The man Stidson only went with him, as far as I can tell, because Micky insisted.'

'Yes,' said Auntie. 'I can see what happened. Stidson was surprised to find how much Michael knew about the secret places and himself. He became nervous and decided to run away, and the only way he could do it was by making the child secure long enough for him to make his plans. Then when he was ready to go he threw the key in to us, knowing that we should soon find somebody who would guide us to the place. I feel sure he did not mean to do the child any harm.'

'No,' said Mummy, and there was an indignant note in her voice as she spoke, 'perhaps not. Fortunately Micky is not a child to be scared into a fit, but some children would have been driven almost crazy shut up in such a place. As it is it makes my blood boil when I think of that child left in the dark in a hut in the middle of a wood like that.'

'It's well over,' said Auntie, trying to smooth Mummy's anger away.

'Yes, but if I ever meet that Stidson again . . . '

'You won't, you may be sure, so why waste your grey matter in getting worked up about him?'

They both watched Micky coming in on the breakers on his surf board. He did it better than any other member of the family. His happy laughter and cries to his brothers and sisters reassured Mummy about him, and soon she had forgotten most of her worries.

They went home hungry, but not too hungry to talk about the rabbiting which they hoped was to take place later in the day.

About three o'clock they set off for the harvest field. Cook had prepared what Micky called a scrumptious tea, and they all took their share of carrying it. When they arrived there was still a good deal of the field to be cut, so they were all eager to be helpful. They asked Mr Martin what they could do.

He gave them a lesson in standing up the sheaves of corn in stooks. It was not such an easy job as it looked, but the Mackies were all eager to try their hands. The three eldest didn't do so badly, but Micky and Elizabeth were very pleased when Mummy called them to help her set out the tea.

The others went on with the job, and although they did not do it in expert fashion they didn't make a terribly bad hand at it. They were heartily glad when they were called to tea, for their arms were aching and their fingers were very sore.

'Ow!' said David, 'I never knew there were so many thistles in the world. Does all corn have thistles growing in it like this?'

Mr Martin heard him and laughed.

'Ah!' he said. 'When I was your age we had no machines to do the work like this. The corn was cut and then we had to go round and pick it up and tie it into sheaves with some of the corn-stalks. Talk about thistles! We knew what thistles were then, I can tell you. My hands were sometimes swollen as big as two. By and by they got hardened to it, and now I don't suppose I should feel it a bit.'

It was nearing sunset when the last patch of corn was cut. For some time previously there had been a few odd rabbits darting out from under the machine, but during the last ten minutes they seemed to run in all directions. There was tremendous shouting from the men and boys who had come from the district around in the hope of capturing some poor bunny for supper. Dogs chased hither and thither, the Mackie children ran here and there until they were almost exhausted.

Mr Martin laughed at their efforts and called out to them to keep at it. Just at the end, when it seemed that the last rabbit had bolted and the men were already counting up their captures, a little one, quite a baby, came hopping along in a bewildered kind of way and Elizabeth made a grab at it. She fell over right on top of it.

'Oh!' she yelled, 'I've caught a rabbit. I've caught a rabbit.'

'Where is it?' shouted Mr Martin.

'I'm lying on it.'

Such a shout of laughter went up from all those who heard what she said.

'There'll be a squashed rabbit on the field then,' said Jean, 'after your weight has been on it.'

Actually the little thing was none the worse and Elizabeth was wild with delight at her success.

'Mummy, do let me keep it and take it home for a pet,' she asked.

After a lot of persuasion Mummy said she might, and she bore it home in triumph, declaring she knew exactly where there was a suitable box to keep it in.

When they arrived at the house Nora met them at the gate.

'Anything the matter, Nora?' asked Mummy.

'I hope not, m'm, but that there boatman, Maclean, has been waiting for you for nearly an hour and he has someone with him.'

'Someone?' queried Auntie. 'Who is the someone?'

'It's a Police Inspector,' said Nora, in a voice which showed how thrilled she was.

'Police Inspector!' cried the children.

'Yes,' said Michael, in a pompous voice. 'I expect he has come to interview me.'

The other children joined in derisive laughter, but Mrs Mackie looked worried, and said, 'Bother!'

CHAPTER XI

Fun at the Flower Show

MICHAEL was severely disappointed because he was not called in to see the Inspector. He hoped against hope until he saw him walking away down the drive. When Mummy came back from showing him out, she said:

'Micky dear, if you should meet either of those men alone and they start asking you questions I want you to dry up as dumb as . . . as . . . '

Mrs Mackie paused for a suitable word.

'I know,' said Elizabeth, 'as dumb as Marjorie.'

Michael almost shrieked his protest at this.

'Marjorie,' he said, 'Marjorie isn't dumb. She talks to me a lot. I know her language.'

'You would,' said Jean, 'understand donkey's language.'

Marjorie was a donkey; one of those very living animal toys that young children delight in. She had been given to Micky at some Christmas or birthday and he had been faithful to her ever since. She invariably went to bed with him, and now that he was growing up he seemed more attached to her than ever. He could not be teased out of his attachment to her.

When he went to the nursing home for an operation Marjorie went, too, and was solemnly carried into the operating theatre where, according to Micky, 'those troublesome tonsils of hers' were removed.

His long conversations with her always sounded very one-sided to the other children, but to him she was as real and as talkative as his friend Peter. Hence his protest when Elizabeth suggested he should be as dumb as Marjorie.

'All right, Mummy,' he said, 'if you want me to say nothing to them I'll be as dumb as Elizabeth's dolls.'

This counter-attack brought a dangerous flash to Elizabeth's eyes, but for once she said nothing.

After the children were all in bed Mrs Mackie told Auntie what had taken place at her interview with the police.

Maclean was not a policeman in disguise, but he was attached to the Customs as what they called a 'special officer'. He had been living as a boatman among the people who were suspected of smuggling. He had been able to establish beyond any doubt that smuggling was carried on and he had compiled a good list of the people he knew were engaged in it.

But he had never been able to discover any of the hiding-places the gang used.

'I can give you information about that,' said Mrs Mackie, 'but if I do, in return you must promise me that my little boy's adventure shall not be brought into it.'

The Inspector protested. 'Isn't there something about the child having been shut up by the man Stidson?'

'I'm saying nothing about that, simply because I will not have my child bothered with the business. I shall never bring any charge against the man on that account.'

There was a good deal of argument until the men realized that Mrs Mackie was not to be moved from her point about Micky. Then they gave way and in return she told them about the box in the hold of the wreck and the one in the hut at Spion Kop.

'There is still one more,' she added, 'but it is in a place you would never find without our assistance. We will take you to it at some convenient time, but for the time being it is quite safe where it is. Nobody can get at it.'

They departed after having asked Mrs Mackie to let nobody touch the box in the secret hiding-place. They were not going to remove the other two but merely set a watch over them.

'It is no good,' said Maclean, 'just capturing the stuff; we must actually catch the men with it in their possession.'

'Well,' said Auntie, when Mummy had finished telling her all about it, 'we seem to have plunged into the middle of an exciting affair.'

'Yes, and I wish we hadn't. It would have been much better for the children if they had had a more ordinary holiday.'

'I don't think it is going to hurt them; they were just crazy for adventure before they came here and now that they are having it they are too sensible to be alarmed by it.'

'Well, anyway, there is one thing I am determined on. There are going to be no interviews with Pressmen, and no evidence given by my children if I can avoid it.'

The following day there was a flower show and carnival of sorts to be held at South Moxton, about twelve miles away, and Mrs Mackie had promised the children that they should all go to it. It turned out a glorious day, and the whole family crammed themselves into the car and motored over.

Years afterwards the Mackies talked over the events of that memorable afternoon, and for once they were all in complete agreement that it was one of the best days of the holiday.

As soon as they arrived Mummy told them they could wander round the show ground and spend their own money as they pleased. The only stipulation was that no child was to be left alone. They were all to meet at the tea tent at 4.30.

'We shall turn up for that all right,' said David.

Of all the Mackies he was the most keen on flowers and animals. Anything in the way of a wee beastie appealed to him, so the first thing he did was to go to the bee-keeping tent where a demonstration was being given. Jean stayed with him, although she was dying to go on the Dodgems.

The lecturer was calmly sitting down among a perfect cloud of bees giving a demonstration of the correct method of handling frames of honeycomb.

'Coo!' said Jean. 'What a nerve!'

A very large country-woman standing beside her said:

'My blessed senses, yes. I wouldn' go in there with them toads not if you was to pay me. They've got hot feet.'

'Toads,' said David; 'they're bees.'

The woman laughed. 'So they be, and don't I know it. I had a swarm come in house once. They flew in bedroom window and pitched right inside my best hat. They did, true's I'm here. I never found 'em till I went to bed at night. I'd left my Sunday hat hanging up, serve me right fer not puttin' 'n away, and when I went up to bed 'twas still middlin' light, so I could see there was something wrong with my hat, seem so. I went and lifted'n off the peg and the weight of'n frightened me so I let'n fall.'

'Were you stung?' asked David, who was already delighted with the story.

'Stung, my young gentleman, I was stung so that I was pretty near double the size I am now.'

David threw a rapid glance over the lady's ample bulk in a way that caused Jean to explode.

'You'm amused, my child, but 'twasn't very amusing for me.'

'I'm sorry,' said Jean, 'I wasn't really laughing at the idea of your being stung.'

Then David set her off again by asking in the most solemn manner, 'If a person swells to twice their usual size does their weight double itself, too.'

The woman looked hard at him, but could not detect the suspicion of a smile on his face.

'I don't know about that,' she said, 'but I was a sight to be seen to be believed, I can tell you.'

'Yes,' said David, 'I can quite imagine it.'

The woman moved away and a gentleman, who had evidently been listening to the conversation, turned to David and looked at him very hard.

'Do you fancy yourself as a funny man?' he said.

'Pardon?' said David, pretending to be both deaf and dense.

The man did not take his eyes from his face.

'What are you going to be when you grow up?' he asked.

'A man,' said David.

'Yes, of course, I know that, seeing you are a boy now.'

'It doesn't always follow.'

'I don't like little boys who try to be smart.'

'Oh! It's no effort,' replied David.

The man was bound to laugh at this, and said:

'What is your name?'

'David Alexander Mackenzie, Daddy wanted a boy called David, and I was born on Alexandra Day and he thought the initials would probably be appropriate.'

'I see, David. Tell me, are you watching this bee demonstration because you want to learn about them?'

'No, not really, but all flying and creeping things are fascinating to me.'

'Is this your sister?'

'Yes, that's Jean.'

'Is she your only sister?'

'No, there are five of us. Daddy calls us his nap hand. He says he is going nap on us every time, and it is up to us to win for him.'

'Win what?'

'Credit, honour, distinction, anything like that,' said Jean.

'Is your Daddy in America now?'

'Yes, how did you guess?'

'I know your Daddy.'

'Do you? Mummy is over here, do come and see her. She will be awfully pleased to meet a friend of Daddy's.'

'Will you introduce me to her?'

'Certainly,' said David.

'How can you? You have not asked me my name yet.'

'No need to, sir. I know it.'

'Do you, indeed? How?'

'There is a corner of your handkerchief sticking out and I can see the name, Simpson, on it.'

The gentleman looked annoyed and then burst out laughing. 'Clever, my son, but wrong. Have you ever heard of a dhobi?'

'Yes, rather. My Daddy was in India once; that's where he met Mummy.'

'Then you know that a dhobi is an Indian washerman.'

'Yes.'

'If you knew as much about dhobis as I do you would know that the name on your handkerchief is nothing as a guide to its ownership.'

'I've heard Mummy tell many tales about Indian dhobis,' said Jean, 'but she herself says she thinks half of them are legends.'

Meanwhile Alan, Micky, and Elizabeth had gone into one of the flower-show tents. The first thing that met them when they went in was a long stand filled with the most luscious-looking apples; apples yellow, apples red, apples green, apples splashed with orange colour; huge great cookers, more modest eaters; pippins and seedlings; all with brightly shining skins.

'My! What apples!' said Elizabeth.

They wandered round until they came to one dish of the most splendid-looking apples they had ever seen. One of them had been split open to show that the inside was as sound as the outside was beautiful. Surmounting them was a blue card bearing the magic words, First Prize.

'Yes, and I should think they deserve it,' said Alan.

There was an oldish man standing gazing at those same apples, and at Alan's comment he made a snorting noise.

'Of course they deserve it,' he said. 'You won't beat they apples in the whole of the county, no, nor all England. I took more care of 'em than I ever did of my own children, I was going to say.'

'I congratulate you on getting first prize with them,' said Elizabeth.

'That's just it, I didn't get no prize at all.'

'But there is a card on it.'

'I can see that as well as you although I'm over seventy. No, Missy, you're too young to know the sort of tricks some people will get up to. Last night those apples were growing in my garden and I had entered them for this class at the show. I thought I'd leave them until this morning and pick them absolutely fresh for sending in. I got up at four o'clock and all the apples was gone. The tree had been stripped in the night and there wasn't a nob left except a few what was no good. There's wickedness for you.'

'Do you mean,' said Alan, amazed, 'that somebody else has shown your apples and taken first prize with them?'

'That's just what I do mean, and if I was a younger man I'd go to the one that done it and let him know who he had to deal with.'

'But what a shame,' said Micky.

The old man hobbled off, muttering to himself, and a much younger man with a mahogany-coloured face spoke to the children.

'Old Silas been telling you the tale?' he asked.

Elizabeth nodded.

'He's told that same tale every year for forty years, but everybody knows him so they take no notice of him. A dirty trick was played on him like that many years ago, and it upset him so that he never got over it. He always tells exactly the same tale, whether it's about apples, pears, peas, potatoes, or anything else. He has always been robbed of his best crop and somebody else has taken the prize with it. He's quite harmless, really, but he does sometimes make strangers believe him. The joke is he lives in town with a married daughter where they have no garden at all.'

The children moved on. Alan said:

'I wonder which of those two was telling the truth.'

He soon received his answer, for at the other side of the tent was the old man holding forth to two ladies about the first prize peas.

'Pinched out of me garden before four o'clock this morning,' they heard him say.

'Poor old chap,' said Micky. 'But there, he doesn't know he's dotty, so what does it matter.'

Elizabeth's attention was next caught by some truly colossal beans. There they were lying in a basket, all exactly the same length and width, and without a blemish on them.

'What beans!' she cried. 'I don't wonder they have the first prize. Aren't they whoppers!'

'Yes,' said a little lady with a sharp nose, who was standing by, 'whoppers they are, and that's all. Beans like that are no good. The judges nowadays give all the prizes for size; it must be the biggest ever. Look at this dish of beans here, they're not nearly so big, but they are much better beans. After all, what are beans for except eating? Those are what I call pantomime beans.'

'Pantomime beans!' laughed Alan. 'What on earth are they?'

'Why, great things like that. Give one of those to a clown in a pantomime or a circus to hit the other clown across the head with and everybody will roar. But as for eating them!'

'Did you grow those smaller ones?' asked Elizabeth innocently.

'Yes,' she replied, 'or my husband did, and that's the same thing.'

'Is it?' said Micky. Then as he moved away he added, 'I wonder if she would say that if her husband was run over by a bus?'

In the next tent they heard an altercation between two women over some eggs. As far as they could make head and tail of it one of them had received first prize for eggs and the other was declaring she shouldn't because the eggs were small.

'They ought to have been weighed,' she declared.

'Yours don't match,' retaliated the other.

Later on they heard a farmer's wife whispering to another woman that the first-prize butter had been bought and had not been made by the woman who had shown it.

'Let's get out of this,' said Alan. 'I have never heard so much envy, hatred, and malice, and all uncharitableness in one afternoon in my life. To listen to all these people you would think that the people of this part of the world were all rogues.'

There was a policeman standing at the door of the tent and he grinned at Alan's indignation.

'Bless you, sir,' he said, 'they don't mean anything by it. It is just a way of letting off steam. They'll all be good friends again tomorrow.'

'And will they say the same about one another again next year?'

'They will, sir. We had a funny thing happen down here last year. A well-known man in the parish offered a special prize of five pounds for the best basket of potatoes of a certain variety. Well, as it happened, his own son entered for the competition, and won the prize. It was all perfectly fair because it was an outside judge, and he didn't know whose potatoes they were. Well, you should have heard the talk that went round. People declared that the man himself had been motoring over half the county searching for the most perfect potatoes he could find, and that he gave them to his son to put in for the show.'

The policeman laughed, and after he had saluted a gentleman who was just passing in, he added:

'But he had his own back on them, though.'

'Did he? How?'

'He gave a bit of a supper and invited all the men who had been in for this potato competition, and when the supper was over he made a bit of a speech, and told them they had just eaten the prize potatoes.'

They left the flower tents and went off to the amusements. The first thing that attracted them was a skittle alley, where a very red-faced man was announcing to all and sundry that there was a pig to be won.

'Oh! Alan,' cried Elizabeth, 'wouldn't it be lovely if you could win a pig.'

'Go on, try for it,' said Micky.

'That's right, sir, three balls for threepence, and best score of the day wins a pig,' shouted the red-faced man.

Alan paid his threepence and took up the first ball. It seemed terribly heavy, but he skittled it along the alley as he had seen the men do. At least he tried to, but it slipped out of his hand, and after a wildly erratic career it took seven pins off the board.

Elizabeth and Micky clapped with delight. The red-faced man looked astonished. 'Two more to get down,' he roared, 'and two balls to do it with.'

Alan was quite nervous as he trundled up the second ball, and it went much slower than he intended, but, by an almost miraculous fluke, he took off the other two pins.

'Nine down with two balls,' bellowed the red-faced man. Crowds of onlookers took up the chorus, and Alan soon found himself the centre of an admiring throng.

'Gimme your name and address,' demanded the ruddy one, 'that'll take a bit of beating, and if you don't win that pig you ought.'

The children dashed off to find Mummy to tell her of Alan's great skittling feat, but she was not to be seen, so they went back to their fun.

They went on the roundabouts and dodgems, shied at cokernuts. It was at the cokernut shies that they were rather scared by a gipsy-looking fellow who had almost forced Alan into throwing. When he hit one cokernut fair and hard in the middle it did not budge and he cried out:

'You must have the beastly things fastened in the cups.'

The man became extremely offensive, and spoke to Alan in such a threatening way that Elizabeth was quite frightened.

They soon forgot that when they heard a man announcing that there were to be sports with special races for children.

'Let's go and see 'em,' said Michael.

'What's the good,' answered Alan, 'you can't run for nuts. None of our family are real runners.'

'I can run,' said Elizabeth. 'If there is a race for little girls I'll enter.'

They went across to see, and found the races did not begin until six o'clock. A baby show was in progress on the sports ground, and the world's fattest babies seemed to have come specially for the occasion. The mothers looked swollen with pride, and the babies looked more swollen with whatever food they had been fed on. They all shone, both mothers and babies.

Four-thirty found them all at the tea tent, and the three children were presented to 'Mr Simpson', whose real name they found was said to be Donaldson.

The moment he looked at him Alan went close to Mrs Mackie and whispered:

'Make some excuse for coming outside for a moment, I want to speak to you urgently.'

CHAPTER XII

Startling Happenings

MRS MACKIE very cleverly managed to get outside with Alan without attracting any notice, and as soon as they were alone she asked:

'What is the matter? Anything gone wrong?'

'I'm not sure, Mummy, but who is this Mr Donaldson?'

'I hardly know. He struck up an acquaintance with Jean and David, and then it turned out that he knows Daddy.'

'Oh! I see. But it seems funny to me.'

'Why does it?'

'Well, a few mornings ago, when I was out riding on Rajah I passed that man, I'm sure it was the same, just along the road near our house. Stidson was with me, and I thought I saw a sort of a glance of recognition between them, although they did not speak. I asked Stidson who this man was, and he said he did not know; said he'd never seen him before.'

'What about it?'

'This; it was a lie.'

'How do you know?'

'Because I had seen Stidson talking to him only the evening before when I was running down to the post. They did not see me, and they didn't hear me because I was running with daps on, but I distinctly heard Stidson say, "Right you are, Charlie." I'm positive it was the same man.'

Mrs Mackie looked a bit perplexed at that, and said:

'But why should he want to make friends with us and say he knows Daddy?'

'We'll soon find out if he really does know Daddy,' replied Alan. 'You leave it to me, Mummy, and if you hear me saying things that sound a bit foolish don't take any notice except to listen to his replies. And will you lend me your camera?'

'I've used the last exposure on my film. What do you want it for?'

'I'd like to get a photo of him, that's all.'

'Sorry, but we can't get a film in the show ground, I'm afraid.'

'Never mind, but I've thought of a good plan to find out if he is a fraud or not.'

'Well, my son, we must go in to tea, or they will be wondering what we are doing.'

When they returned to the tent Mr Donaldson, or Simpson, or whatever his name was, was talking to the children about their house and asking all sorts of questions. Was it haunted? Had it any secret passages? He had heard that most old houses had. Micky, of course, was terribly eager to tell him of all their discoveries, but a fearful hack on the shin from Jean stopped him in time, and he very nearly cried aloud with the pain.

When the man noticed his red face, he said:

'What's the matter, old man? Something stung you?'

'No,' said Micky, 'but I think I've got a pain.'

'You think you have; I think I should know if I had one.'

'You'll stop and have tea with us, won't you, Mr Donaldson?'

'No, thank you, Mrs Mackie; I don't think I must stop. It is very kind of you, but . . .'

'Well, before you go,' said Alan, 'I should like to get a snap of you to send to Daddy; just to remind him of an old friend.'

'No, no, no, I wouldn't think of it. I hate having my photo taken at any time, and I can hardly call your father an old friend. I just know him; that's all.'

'Did you know him in India?' asked Alan, with a perfectly innocent face.

'Yes, that's where I met him first.'

'Would that be when he was stationed at Amballa or at Peshawar?'

'At Amballa.'

'Curious,' said Alan, with a quick look at his mother.

'Why?'

'I mean curious that we should meet like this.'

'Oh! Yes, quite.'

'I'll remember you to Daddy when I write.'

As Alan said this he levelled the camera at the man and quickly clicked the shutter. 'Thank you,' he said.

A flush of fierce anger passed over the man's face. He turned to Mrs Mackie and said, in an angry voice:

'I asked your child not to photograph me. I hate it. I shall be glad if you will promise me to have the film destroyed without being printed.'

The other children looked amazed but Auntie sensed what was going on, and said:

'Are you afraid of having your photo taken?'

'Afraid? Certainly not, but I just detest it; that's all.'

'I suppose,' said Mummy, sweetly, 'there is always a danger of your photo getting into the wrong hands.'

'I'm afraid I don't understand you, madam.'

'I think you do, Mr ... ? Simpson, is it? Or shall we still say Donaldson?'

'I'll wish you good afternoon,' he said turning away with a very uncomfortable look.

'By the by,' called Alan. 'You might be interested to know that my Daddy never was in either Amballa or Peshawar in his life. He told me so.'

As soon as they were setting about tea, Auntie asked:

'What was the meaning of that little bit of play-acting?'

'I think we won't say much about it at present,' said Mrs Mackie, quietly.

'There's only one thing that I'm sorry about,' said Alan, 'and that is that there was no film in the camera.'

'Then why on earth did you pretend to take a snap of him, if you knew that?' demanded David.

'I wanted him to think I had done it. I have an idea he was really very much in earnest when he said he objected to having his photo taken. I don't think he would care for the police to have a copy.'

Of course all the children wanted to know why not, but Mummy urged them to get on with their tea, and there was

no more said for a while, until David spoke through a mouth-
ful of creamy bun.

'I thought he was a very nice chap.'

'You would,' said Alan. 'Don't speak with your mouth full.'

'It isn't full.'

'No, it's so big that . . . '

'That'll do,' insisted Mummy. 'Hurry on with your tea.
You won't be able to stay very late, so you must do all that
you are going to do in the fair.'

They required no further urging, and soon they were off
to the fray once more. This time Mummy ordained that
they should keep all together, and she and Auntie followed
not far behind.

Micky was terribly anxious to win some gold-fish.

'You see,' he said, 'Adolphus has died, so we must have
another to take his place.'

Adolphus was the gold-fish they had had for more than
two years. He was the only survivor of three, and he had led
a very placid existence until on one of the hottest days of the
lovely summer of 1933 he died. His bowl had accidentally
been left in a very blazing spot, and the heat had been too
much for him. As David put it, he had been boiled. So
Michael would not rest until he had another fish to take the
place of the late lamented Adolphus.

Auntie offered to buy him one. 'It will be much cheaper,'
she said, 'than throwing those wretchedly erratic ping-pong
balls until you win one.'

'Think so?' said Micky, in his cheekiest manner. 'You just
watch me.'

The very first ball he threw went unerringly to the spot,
and the showman handed him a bowl of fish without even
speaking. The other children were so elated at Micky's
success that they wanted to try, and the man naturally urged
them to do so, but Mummy very tactfully drew their attention
to something else.

'If I hadn't done so,' she said to Auntie afterwards, 'they
would have wasted so much money that the fish we had

captured would have cost about six times what they were worth.'

Alan led them on to the skittle alley, where he was anxious to see if his record still stood.

The red-faced man bellowed a welcome, when he saw him. 'Come on, sir, see if you can do it again.'

'No fear,' said Alan, who was not anxious to show anyone what a fluke his first effort had been. 'Auntie, you have a go.'

'Yes, Auntie, do,' was the cry from all the Mackies including Mummy.

'That's right, Auntie,' roared the ruddy one, 'show the kids what you can do.'

Auntie blushed a little at the attention she was attracting, but she paid her money and had her throw. The alley had become the centre of a delighted throng of country folk on holiday, all eager to see the pig won.

Auntie sent down her first ball, and it went straight and true right through the pins without touching one.

'Rotten shot,' yelled Micky.

'Be quiet, you rude boy,' chided Elizabeth.

'Well, so it was a rotten shot.'

Auntie took her second ball, and after listening carefully to the advice of a young farmer standing by hurled her second ball. Yes, hurled is the right word, for it sped to the far end of the alley without touching the boards once, over the top of the pins, and ended up by tearing a hole in the canvas at the back.

'Hi! Missis,' shouted someone, 'you baint playing baseball, you know.'

'Be careful,' said another, 'or you'll catch somebody 'pon the napper next time.'

'My days!' said a third, 'I'm glad she don't backfire.'

By this time Auntie's face was scarlet, but she was determined not to be jeered out of trying with her last ball. Another man offered to throw for her, but she said, 'I can do it myself, thank you,' in a very auntieish kind of voice, and stooped once more for the fray. What happened no one exactly knew, but the heavy ball flew off at a tangent and caught the red-faced man full in the watch-chain.

He doubled up as though he had been charged by a hippopotamus, and let out a long string of gasping grunts. The colour of his face became alarmingly vivid, but the spectators were not the least bit frightened. They howled with delight. People came running from the farthest corners of the fairground to cheer. They had no notion what they were cheering about, but seeing scores of people doubled up with convulsive laughter they roared with them.

Auntie's state of embarrassment was dreadful. She wanted to laugh and she almost wanted to cry. She wanted to apologize to the man she had laid out and she wanted to run away. She wanted to face the people who were having such sport at her expense, and she wanted to hide herself for a week.

The Mackies had to hold one another up, they were so helpless with laughter. David at last lay on the ground and rolled as though in agony. Mummy was vexed but almost hysterical with suppressed laughter.

At last the injured man rose from the ground where he had been sitting and began to laugh himself.

'Look here,' he cried, 'no more of your aunties for me. They'm too strong.'

'Come along, we had better get away from here,' said Mummy; 'we are getting too much publicity for my liking.'

After Auntie had apologized to the man of red visage, and he had assured her that no real harm was done, they moved away, but as they went they could still hear his voice above all other noises exhorting folk to come and win a pig.

'He's none the worse, evidently,' said Jean.

They next moved to a stand where a conjurer was preparing to give an exhibition of his skill.

'Oo! Mummy, do let's stop and see him,' said Elizabeth. 'I do love conjurers.'

They paid only threepence each for a front seat and did not have to wait long for the show to commence. The man did a number of the usual tricks that the children had seen scores of times, and then he announced that he was going to show them a new one that he had learnt from a famous Egyptian illusionist.

'For this,' he said, 'I shall want the help of a little boy. Will somebody . . .?'

He had not time to finish the sentence before David had hopped up on to the little stage.

'Ah!' he cried, 'here is a young gentleman come to assist me.'

He drew forward a chair and said, 'Sit down there, will you please?'

David sat down and his family watched very eagerly to see what he would be called upon to do.

'Now,' said the conjurer, 'will some lady or gentleman lend me a shilling? Nobody? Has nobody got a shilling to lend me?'

No one was at all eager to lend him a shilling, so at last he said, 'Very well, I shall have to use one of my own.'

He took a shilling from his pocket and then to David he said, 'Have you a handkerchief?'

'Yes,' said David, 'I think so.' He dived down into his pocket and started pulling out all sorts of things.

'He hasn't got one,' whispered Jean.

'I hope it's clean if he has,' said Mummy.

After he had removed string, cigarette cards, half a copy of some weekly paper such as his soul loved, a large lump of wood that he had started to carve into the shape of a racing motor, he came to the hanky. It was so surprisingly clean that Mummy let out a startled 'Good gracious!'

'Now,' said the conjurer, 'I will wrap this shilling in the little boy's handkerchief and put it into his pocket, so.'

He thrust his hand into David's pocket, the inside one of his coat, and then told David to button his coat over so that no one could get at it.

'Right!' said David, with a grin.

'Now,' said the man, 'while I am waiting for my magic to work I must do another trick.'

He then proceeded to do a very common trick, producing an extraordinary number of coloured silk handkerchiefs from nowhere, apparently. Everyone was so intent on watching him that no one noticed David, who appeared to be sitting quite still, with his attention on the silk handkerchiefs. At last the man turned to him and said,

'You haven't let anybody touch my shilling, have you?'

'No.'

'Sure?'

'Quite sure.'

'Then take out the handkerchief and give it to me.'

David put his hand into his pocket and withdrew the wrapped-up handkerchief.

'Now open it,' said the conjurer, 'and show the people that you have my shilling safe and sound.'

David stepped to the front of the stage and in full view of everybody opened out the hanky. There was nothing in it. The man looked puzzled and the audience laughed. A man called out, 'Any fool can do that trick.'

David shook out the handkerchief in front of the faces of the audience, but the conjurer thrust his hand into the pocket rather roughly. David grinned up at him saucily.

'You'll never find it,' he said.

'What have you done with my shilling?'

'The shilling's in your pocket where I saw you put it,' he said.

There was a loud laugh at this, and when it had subsided he called out:

'Ladies and gentlemen, allow me to show you MY trick.'

He put his hand to his trousers pocket and very gingerly drew out another hanky, which he carefully unfolded and took from it a tiny fluffy live chicken.

'You little brat,' muttered the man, just loud enough for David to hear.

The audience, including the Mackies, was a bit mystified until when they were outside David explained.

'I had two hankies,' he said, 'and when the man put the

one back in my pocket I knew the shilling wasn't there, but something else was. I've seen a trick like it before. Then when I saw how closely everyone was watching the man and not me I ever so carefully felt my pocket and knew that there was something alive there. By pretending to fold my arms I was able to get the one hanky out and the other in that inside pocket. Then bit by bit I managed to get the other into my trousers pocket. I had only just that second finished when he turned to me.'

'But the audience didn't know how you had fooled him.'

'No, but I did, and so did he,' said David, delighted at the success of his trick.

'Rather weak, I call it,' said Elizabeth.

'You couldn't have done it, anyway.'

'Rather mean to spoil the man's trick for him, I think,' said Jean.

When they left the conjuring they wandered round the ground until they were all beginning to get a bit tired.

'Now for home,' said Mummy, at last.

'Oh! Mummy,' cried Alan, 'can't I stop to see if I have won my pig?'

'Your pig! You seem very certain of it. If you like you can go and ask the man what time the name of the winner will be announced.'

Alan hurried off, and when his old friend saw him he shouted, 'What have you done with Auntie? Don't bring her back here any more; I haven't got my breath back properly yet.'

'You needn't fear; she's had enough.'

'H'm! So have I.'

'What time will the winner of the pig be announced?'

'Ten o'clock.'

'Not till then?'

'No, we shall do most of our business between now and then. See how the crowds are coming in.'

'My mother will never let me stop till ten o'clock.'

'Well, never mind. I've got your name and address, and if you win the pig you will receive a letter and you can go across to Farmer Gurney's and claim it.'

Alan went back to his mother a little disappointed. As he expected, she refused to go home without him, and also refused to wait till ten o'clock. A last turn on the dodgems for all of them, and then they crowded into the car for the journey home.

Just as Mrs Mackie was getting into the driver's seat half a dozen tough fellows raced past, shouting at one another, and indulging in some very boisterous play. They dodged round the Mackie's car and nearly knocked Mummy over. As soon as they had chased away again she said:

'I thought that sort of thing didn't happen in England.'

'There is always plenty of hooliganism at these country fairs,' replied Auntie.

'I don't mean that.'

'Then what do you mean?'

'That wasn't just horse-play; that was carefully arranged. They had my camera.'

'What! Stole it?'

'Yes, snatched it out of my hand.'

'That's too bad. Aren't you going to complain to the police?'

'Oh, Mummy!' cried Alan. 'Don't you see, they were put to that by Simpson or Donaldson, or whoever he is, because he thought I had taken his photo.'

'That is just what I mean when I say I thought that sort of thing didn't happen in England. I only associated that kind of trick with the wild and woolly west.'

'There's a police sergeant, over there,' said Jean. 'Won't you make a complaint?'

'No,' said Mummy, 'we are going home.'

All the way home she was very quiet and thoughtful, and the children did all the talking. They usually did, but to-night they were full of excitement and talked about hold-ups and robberies, skittle competitions, catching runaway pigs, conjuring tricks they had seen, the furious bumps they had

had on the dodgems, the fat lady who was stung to twice her usual size, and a hundred other things.

Home at last and the children, except Alan, hurried off to their baths and beds. Alan was tremendously thrilled when Mummy whispered to him:

'I am going back to the fair presently, and I want you to come with me. Daddy is not here, so you must take his place and be my champion.'

'What are you going to do?'

'Look for Mr Donaldson-Simpson and draw the attention of the police to him.'

'I expect he has disappeared by now.'

'Never mind, I'm going to look for him.'

CHAPTER XIII

Alan Wins a Prize

It was nearly half past nine by the time Mrs Mackie and Alan arrived back in the fair ground. It was then getting quite dark and all the stalls, shows, and roundabouts were bright with hissing arc lamps. The whole place was so thronged with people that it was almost impossible to move. Mummy would not take her car into the car park of the show but had left it at a garage in the main street of South Moxton.

'What are you going to do first of all?' asked Alan.

'I am going to the show secretary's tent to inform them of the loss of my camera.'

They soon found the tent and a very pleasant-faced gentleman rose at Mummy's entrance.

'Good evening, Mrs Mackie,' he said. 'Is there anything I can do for you?'

'Good evening, Colonel Ridler,' replied Mummy. 'Have you a minute or two to spare me?'

'Certainly. I can leave affairs to my assistant for a little while. In fact, I shall be glad to get out into the air a bit. Is this your son?'

'Yes, Colonel Ridley; this is my eldest boy, Alan.'

'How do you do, Alan? Enjoying the fun of the fair?'

'Yes, thank you, sir. I hope I may have won a pig.'

'What, at the skittles?'

'Yes,' said Mummy, 'he had the world's most wonderful fluke. But we must not take up your time with things like that. What I really came about was this. A man, calling himself Donaldson, struck up an acquaintance with my children in the flower-show this afternoon. He told them he knew my husband. In a very short while we proved he didn't because Alan floored him completely by asking if he knew Daddy at Amballa. He said he did, but as my husband had never been to Amballa in his life we suspected this man. Alan, to make matters doubly sure, said he would take his photo so that he might send Daddy a copy. The man objected very strongly, and when Alan did actually pretend to snap him he was furious.'

'Strange,' said the Colonel.

'But that's not the strangest part. Just before I started for home with the children a gang of roughs chased round my car and almost knocked me off my feet. As they did so I felt one of them snatch at my camera. He went off with it, and I have not seen it since.'

'Wait a bit. A young man came to the secretary's tent about an hour ago and brought in a camera which he said he had picked up just outside the car park. Perhaps it is yours.'

'Perhaps it is,' said Mrs Mackie. 'May I see?'

'Of course.'

They re-entered the tent and the colonel said:

'What have you done with that camera which was brought in just now?'

'Here it is, sir.'

'Thank you. Is that yours, Mrs Mackenzie?'

Mummy looked at it very carefully. 'Yes,' she said, 'that is mine. I am quite sure of it. Look, I scratched my initials just there. There they are, A.M.M.'

'Definitely your camera,' said the Colonel. 'I am very glad you have it back, but sorry you should have lost it in such an unpleasant way.'

'You notice,' said Alan, 'that the film has been removed.'

'Why, so it has!'

Mrs Mackie opened the camera. The film had been carefully taken out, but inside was a scrap of paper on which had been written in pencil, 'Thank you. Sorry for the inconvenience.'

'Well, dear me,' said Colonel Ridler, 'I think this is a case for the police.'

'So do I,' said Mummy.

'Inspector Snelgrove is here somewhere. Go and see if you can find him, George, will you?'

'Yes, sir,' said the man, and hurried off.

While they were waiting the colonel was very busy receiving money from stall-holders and ticket sellers, issuing prize certificates, answering a thousand questions, and doing all the jobs that fall to the lot of the secretary of a big show.

Alan and Mummy talked quietly at one side of the tent.

'How did you know this colonel, Mummy?'

'I met him at the Rectory garden party last week. He knows some people I know in India, and his wife called to see me a day or two later.'

Very soon George reappeared, followed by the same police inspector who had called to interview Mummy with the man Maclean.

'Good evening, madam,' he said. 'I did not think we should meet again so soon.'

'Ah! Inspector,' said the Colonel. 'You have met Mrs Mackenzie before, have you?'

'Yes, Colonel. We have had a little business together. Now what can I do for you?'

'Well, really, I am a bit confused about it,' said the Colonel, 'but no doubt the lady will explain. I am very busy for the next hour, so you will excuse me. If I can be of any assistance please let me know.'

'Thank you,' said Mummy, and she and Alan wished him good night.

They then retired with Inspector Snelgrove to the back of the largest flower marquee, where they related once again the whole story of the incidents connected with the camera. He heard them through without interrupting. When Mrs Mackie had finished, he said:

'Will you be good enough to lend me the camera and the piece of paper with that message. We might get something out of that.'

'Do you mean finger-prints?' asked Alan.

'Yes, and other things.'

'What other things?'

'Never mind, sonny. Now, can you give me a description of this man who calls himself Donaldson?'

'Don't forget,' said Alan, 'that he had the name Simpson on his handkerchief.'

'Simpson, did you say?'

'Yes, didn't we tell you?'

'No, but it does not help me at all. Just describe him to me.'

They gave the Inspector as full a description as they could of the man, and he thanked them, and said he would soon make inquiries about him.

'There is no doubt in my mind,' he said, 'he deliberately got talking to your children for a purpose.'

'What purpose?' asked Mummy.

'I don't know. But you say he was asking about secret passages and things like that.'

'Yes.'

'Well, keep your eyes open, and if you ever see him again let me know as quickly as possible. He is probably far away from here by now, so you won't be likely to see him tonight.'

It was after ten o'clock when their interview with the Inspector was finished, and some of the shows were already packing up. The roundabouts were crowded and the dodgems were so full that people were only getting very short rides and the price had been doubled since the earlier part of the evening.

Alan was drawn like a magnet to the skittle alley. The last throw had just taken place, and he and Mummy arrived just in time to hear their ruddy friend bawling out:

'Nine pins down with two balls by two competitors: Mister Tom Gazzard, of Temlecombe, and Master Alan Mackenzie, of Oxmouth Manor. Those two gentlemen, if we can get hold of them, will have to throw again to decide who shall have the pig. There he is, a nice little fat 'un. Tom Gazzard and Alan Mackenzie to throw against one another. I wish I could find 'em both.'

'I be 'ere,' bellowed a voice close to Alan.

'Tom Gazzard's here,' came the shout from a dozen people.

Alan looked round and saw the said Tom. He was about six feet three and a great muscular man.

'Oh! Mummy,' he said, 'it will be useless trying to throw against that giant.'

'Brains are better than brawn,' said Mummy, encouragingly. 'Don't forget David killed Goliath.'

Alan laughed, but it was with rather a nervous voice that he called out: 'I'm here, too.'

'The boy's here,' several men shouted.

Red-face roared his welcome. 'Come along, my little bantam. Come and show them how to do it.'

He winked elaborately at the men crowding round. The mighty Tom looked down at Alan and laughed.

'Be I goin' to throw 'gainst you?' he asked.

'Yes,' said Alan.

'All right, then,' he said. 'You can throw first.'

'No,' insisted Alan. 'You have first go; you ought to let me go last if I want to.'

'Go on, sonny, show me what I've got to beat, and I'll soon beat it.'

Alan appealed to the bystanders.

'Oughtn't he to go first?'

'Get on, Tom,' shouted some of his companions, 'throw and then let the kid throw afterwards.'

'Why should I?'

'Well, he's only a kid.'

'Never mind; he got nine down with two balls, same as I did.'

'Well you ought to give way to a little 'un.'

'Let he give way to a big 'un.'

'I can be as stubborn as you,' said Alan.

The man held an enormous fist in front of Alan's nose.

'See that?' he asked. 'Now, throw first, if you're wise.'

There was a growling chorus of disapproval at Tom's behaviour, and red-face came pushing through to see what was the matter. Twenty people started talking at once.

'Shut up,' he bellowed, and then turning to Mrs Mackie, he said:

'What's the argument about?'

'This man is insisting that my boy should throw first, and he doesn't see why he should; neither do I.'

'Tom,' he roared. 'Haven't you enough sport in you to let the boy go last? Surely you aren't afraid of his beating you.'

'I've as much right to last throw as he has.'

'Do you insist on that right?'

'Yes.'

Turning to Alan, he said: 'Do you?' Here he gave a huge and heavy wink.

'I do.'

'Right! You must toss for it.'

He dived into his capacious pocket and drew out a half a crown. Turning once more to Alan he said: 'Toss that and let Tom call.'

Alan spun the coin high and Tom shouted 'Tails.'

The half-crown fell to the ground, and a ring of spectators thrust their faces forward. 'It's heads,' they shouted.

'You got to go first, Tom, after all,' said red-face, quickly picking up his half-crown. There was a good deal of clapping at that, and Tom flushed angrily, and he muttered to himself.

The pins were placed and Tom spat in his great hard hand. He took the first ball, and with the action of one who had played skittles all his life sent down a ball which took the front pin nicely on the side and carried away that and four others. Another one rocked, but finally decided to stand upright.

'Put that one back on its spot,' Tom called.

'No,' roared the chorus of onlookers, 'it mustn't be touched.'

Tom was getting more and more angry. He threw his next ball with unnecessary force and removed two pins only, leaving the two outsiders still standing.

'Can't get 'em all now, Tom,' volunteered a very old man from the crowd.

'Can't I?' he shouted, hurling the last ball with terrific force, hoping apparently to shake both pins off their feet by the shock of his violence. The result was what might have been expected, he missed them both.

'Seven,' shouted red-face. 'Stick 'em up again, Harry.'

Then to Alan, he said: 'Good luck, sonny.'

The close attention of such a large crowd made Alan very nervous indeed, but he caught a smile from Mummy, and he determined to do his very best; more he could not do. In a remarkable silence he trundled up his first ball. It seemed to travel quite slowly compared with the hurricane rushes of Tom's deliveries. It took away six pins, and there was a shout of approval from the company.

'Well done, little 'un,' said one. 'Play steady,' said another. 'He's a good kid,' cried a third. 'Better to play crafty than all that bombardment,' said yet another.

Alan sent up his next ball, but he knew before it had gone half-way that it was a bad one. There was a groan from the crowd and a jeering cry from Tom when it was seen that he had missed altogether.

'That's a bit too crafty,' sneered Tom.

'Don't you take any notice of him, sonny,' said the ancient one.

With a thumping heart Alan took the last ball. He stooped and sent the ball with more speed this time. It flew straight to one of the pins, knocked it sideways so that it hit over another, and the ball itself cannoned off and removed the third.

A mighty cheer went up. Alan danced with delight. Mummy was equally delighted, although she certainly did not want a live pig. Red-face roared his congratulations, and the crowd started to tease Tom about being beaten by a youngster. He did not wait, however, but started to push his way through the mob.

Alan jumped across and seized his coat. 'Come back a minute,' he said.

The man looked at Alan's red and happy face and his anger seemed to disappear at once. He held out his hand.

'Shake,' he said. 'You beat me fair.' Then, after a pause, he added, 'But I'd like to throw with you again.'

'You would win every time,' said Alan, 'but I want you to do something for me.'

'What's that?'

'I want you to take the pig.'

'Take it? Take it where?'

'I want you to have it. I have no use for it and I expect you have. I'll give it to you.'

Again Tom shook Alan's hand until he almost yelled with the pain.

'You're a sport, you are,' he said. 'Why were you so keen on winning it if you didn't really want it?'

'Just because I was determined to beat you if I could.'

'Well, thank you very much. I did want that pig, wanted it badly.'

'And now it's yours.'

As Tom went to collect the pig, which was sleeping quite peacefully in a little fold nearby, Mummy said to Alan:

'I'm glad you won it, but proud that you could be so generous to the man who lost.'

'Well, you see, Mummy, I won, and that was the thing. But I could see he really wanted that pig and well, what could I have done with it?'

Some of the spectators were frankly dumbfounded.

'My!' said one. 'He's bin and give the pig away.'

'Yes, after winning it, too. I wouldn't, would you?'

'No, I wouldn't, but what I can't understand is why he was so determined to win, as he was, if he never wanted no pig.'

'That's because you can't understand much,' said red-face.

Alan and Mummy were making for the car to return home when there was a tremendous commotion and much shouting. Men and women were running and there were cries of 'There he goes!'

'What is it?' asked Alan. 'Have they caught our thief?'

'No,' laughed Mummy. 'It is your skittling friend. He is chasing his pig which does not appear to want to go with him.'

So it was. The pig had taken fright when Tom had come to claim him, and had bolted through the legs of sundry on-lookers, upsetting not a few.

Loud squeals and grunts marked the progress of the pig

round the show-ground, and in less than two minutes it seemed that the poor, frightened creature had a thousand people after it, led by Tom Gazzard, its new owner.

'Never saw such a steeple-chaser of a pig in my life,' said a gentleman to Alan.

Suddenly the pig doubled back and was headed towards the roundabouts. Finding itself cornered with no way of escape, it jumped on to the lowest platform of the galloping horses just as it was gathering speed. The stupid thing scrambled up higher to the intense amusement of the lingering crowds and amid the shrieks of the maidens who were going round on their wooden cocks and horses. Finally, the pig stood in a kind of tipsy attitude with its feet apart, dazed by the circular movement.

One of the showmen made a noose in a rope and came up behind it, and slipped it over its head. Just at that instant the music of the steam organ started a fresh tune and startled the animal into new life. It jumped down again and jerked the showman off his feet, but its new bid for liberty was of no avail for it ran straight into the arms of the waiting and breathless Tom.

He bore it struggling away and the crowd soon found other amusements.

The journey home was rather slow, because Mrs Mackie was a little nervous of night driving. Consequently, it was quite late when they turned into the drive. As they did so the beam of their headlights showed the crouching figure of a man who darted through the hedge.

'Who was that?' said Mummy, stopping the car.

'Somebody who did not want to be seen,' said Alan.

'Did you recognize him?'

'No, but he seemed a bit familiar.'

'Yes, can't you place him?'

'It was rather like . . . yes, I know, Stidson.'

'That's what I thought.'

'What are you going to do, Mummy?'

'We can't go chasing him. We'll hurry home and I'll ring up Inspector Snelgrove.'

'I wonder if it really is Stidson?'

'Anyway, it is somebody who was very anxious not to be seen, and he was just coming in the direction of our house, so he must be some sort of trespasser.'

They were in the house with the car put safely away in a very few minutes, and while Alan told Auntie the events of the evening Mrs Mackie rang up the police and asked to speak to Inspector Snelgrove.

He was not available at the moment, but Mrs Mackie left a message that she would like him to ring her up when he came in.

'Since you have been gone,' said Auntie, 'I have been having my little adventure.'

'Have you. How thrilling!' said Alan. 'Do tell us.'

'I have had a visitor.'

'Really! Who was it?'

'I can't say.'

'What do you mean?'

'Well, after you had gone, Cook asked if she and Nora might take a walk down into the village. I told them they could go, and said I would look after the house while they were gone. They hadn't departed five minutes before there was a ring at the front-door bell. I went to see who it was, and quite a pleasant-looking man was there. I asked him what he wanted, and he said he had a rather long story to tell so might he come in.'

'Did you let him in?'

'Yes, and I am very glad I did.'

'Why?'

'He had brought a message.'

'Who from?'

'I am not at liberty to say.'

'What do you mean?'

'Well, he told me to say nothing.'

'Auntie, don't be absurd.'

There was an amused look in Auntie's face all the time, and Alan said:

'Come on; you are hiding something. Tell us the joke.'

'Listen,' said Auntie, in a mysterious voice. 'I think I can hear somebody moving about upstairs.'

They listened quietly and they could hear a stealthy footstep descending the stairs.

'Who . . . ?' began Alan, but Mummy darted out of the room into the hall. 'Darling!' she called.

Alan rushed out after her when he heard the tone of her voice.

'Oh! Daddy,' he cried, 'What a fright you did give me!'

'But what has brought you back so soon?'

'Only a flying visit, my dears; I have to meet some people in London tomorrow and then go back again on Tuesday. But I'll go now if you don't want me.'

'Daddy!' they both cried.

A voice came from the top of the stairs.

'Did I hear somebody say Daddy was here?'

CHAPTER XIV

A Valuable Capture

THE following day, however tired Daddy might have been, there was to be no rest for him. The children all trooped into his room at various times and in various stages of dress and undress. Shortly after seven he had the whole lot of them disposed about sundry parts of the bed and room all trying at once to tell him all that Mummy had already told him. In addition, they all wanted to ask about three or four thousand questions, but when he let it out that he had been brought from Southampton by aeroplane he was almost submerged under a torrent of requests for information.

What sort of plane was it? Who piloted him? Did he enjoy it? Where did he land? The answer to this question brought on a new avalanche of talking. On that big field at the back? And they never saw him come?

'I thought I heard a plane,' said Michael, 'and said to David that it seemed jolly close.'

Alan was looking out of the window. 'Do you mean that field there?' he asked.

'Yes.'

'The plane isn't there now.'

'No, I'm sorry to disappoint you, but it had to go back at once.'

'Is it coming to fetch you when you go away?'

'Again I'm sorry to dash your hopes to the ground, but when I leave I shall drive over to Sidford and get in an ordinary vulgar train.'

'Oh!' said Jean. 'Train travel is no longer vulgar; all the best people are going back to the railway for travel. There is no longer any room on the roads so the train is coming into its own again.'

In the end Daddy cut short all the chatter by saying:

'Now, look here. I have only one day with you and I want to

make the most of it, so the best thing you can do is to trot off
and leave me to get up. We'll have one great and glorious
day enjoying ourselves.'

The day was given up to the full enjoyment of the sun and
sea. Daddy said he had been to so many meetings and junket-
ings during his short stay in America (and he had to go back
to it) that he wanted a day of bliss such as only England and his
own family could give him.

Of course he had heard all about the adventures they had
had, and he was very angry when he heard how Micky had
been locked up.

'I only wish I could meet the fellow who did it,' he said.

'He's a big chap,' said Alan, cheekily.

Daddy smiled. 'I think I heard something from Mummy
about you having a tussle with a very big chap and beating
him.'

'Yes, but that was only a game.'

'Never mind, the principle is the same.'

Immediately after breakfast Daddy had to be taken all
round the place to see if he approved of all the things they
had done to improve it. He was very delighted with everything.

'I am just longing for the time when I can come and have
a holiday here myself,' he said.

Everything was inspected; the house, the gardens, the
poultry, the horse, the stream, the pond, everything.

'You are the orderly officer going round on your daily
rounds,' said David, 'and I'm the orderly sergeant.'

'Disorderly, you mean,' snapped Jean.

Mummy came upon the scene. 'Now,' she said, 'you children can have Daddy this morning, but this afternoon he is
my property, so just take notice.'

'Bathing costumes,' said Daddy. 'You must show me what
progress you have made with your swimming.'

Soon they were all on the beach. They bathed and rode
their surf-boards, they swam and dived, they ducked Daddy
and he paid them out by chasing them and holding them

under one by one, until they were all spluttering and choking with seawater.

When they were tired of that they had a great game of tip and run with a piece of wood and a tennis ball. Everybody smote their hardest, ran their fastest, fielded their keenest, and threw in their hardest. Daddy had such a furious innings that he exhausted himself and had to retire for a rest.

Then they took him round to all their rock pools in which they had various fish that they knew by name. One was called Austin, another Radmilovic, another Old Pybus, another they had named Bernard Shaw; there was Osbert . . . Daddy was pinched because he asked, 'Does he sit well?' . . . Epstein, Claude, Ramsay, Trotsky, and Mollison. All these little fishes were recognized and called by their names. The children spent their happiest hours pottering about these pools and searching for fresh fish to name.

This Sunday morning was notable because in a comparatively shallow pool, where they had never found a fish before, they discovered a new one.

'What shall we call him?' was the cry.

All sorts of suggestions were made, and each one was unanimously rejected by all those who had not suggested it. At last it was agreed that Daddy should name this one, and he was ordered to think of something good.

For a time Daddy was stumped. 'H'm, let me think. H'm! . . . H'm!'

'You've said that three times,' said Elizabeth.

'Yes, my child, that is the sound of my thinking engine misfiring.'

In the most tantalizing silence they waited for Daddy to produce his brain wave. At last he said.

'I think we'll call it Ariel.'

'Why?'

'Because it has come unto these yellow sands.'

A rocky silence greeted this effort.

'Shakespeare . . . *The Tempest*, you know,' said Daddy.

'If you are going to take a name from *The Tempest*,' said Alan, who had been reading it at school last term, 'he ought to be called Caliban, I should think. He is much too ugly for Ariel.'

'I know,' replied Daddy. 'We'll call him Trinculo; he looks as though he had been drinking out of Stephano's bottle.'

So Trinculo he was called and Trinculo he remained.

By the time they were ready to return home Alan had made a suggestion that was approved by everybody, that Daddy should be taken home through the rocky tunnel and the priest's hole.

'Yes, I want to see all that,' he said.

'But it will need somebody to go up the other way and open the window-seat to let us out,' remarked Jean.

'Then you can go and do it,' replied David.

There was so much argument about it that at last Daddy cut it short by saying:

'Alan and Jean will come with me and show me the way. the other three can go home through the house and do whatever is necessary to let us out.'

Loud protests! But Daddy insisted on that arrangement and so it was done.

He was frankly amazed at what he was shown and entered the tunnel with a curious feeling of unexplained nervousness.

'Oughtn't we to have a light?' he asked. 'It will be pitch dark in here.'

'I thought of that,' said Alan. 'I brought a torch in my pocket. It is not a very good one, but it will give us enough light, I think.'

Alan led the way, Daddy came next, and Jean brought up the rear, hanging on to Daddy's coat-tails. Their progress was slow because Mr Mackie kept on stopping to examine the walls. At last they reached the door into the priest's hole and found it shut.

'The kids must have got there first and opened before we are ready,' said Alan. 'We shall have to wait a bit and then when they find we are not ready they will shut their end and this will open.'

'What is this little passage on the right?' asked Daddy.

'That is where I got myself shut in. You had better not go in, or when they open this door you'll be stuck there, as I was.'

'Yes, but you'll know I am in there and you will know how to get me out.'

'Very well,' said Alan. 'Take my torch and don't be many seconds!'

'Right!'

Mr Mackie squeezed his way into the little passage and left the two children in complete darkness. He was not gone three minutes, and when he came out his voice sounded a little bit shaky.

'Horrid place to be shut in,' he said.

'Don't I know it,' said Alan. 'I was there for hours and it seemed like weeks.'

At that moment the door in front of them began to open and they immediately passed into the priest's hole. As they entered they were all startled by a flash of light that came right across their faces.

'What are you doing?' called Alan, thinking it was David come down to meet them, but the feeble ray of his own torch was just enough to show him that it was a man he had to deal with and not David at all.

For answer he was thrown violently to one side.

'Look out!' he yelled. Jean screamed, but Daddy quickly placed himself in the doorway leading to the tunnel. Suddenly someone charged furiously at him and nearly had him to the ground, but he had taken the precaution of gripping the sides of the doorway.

'Light, Alan!' he shouted, as he grappled with his attacker.

Alan, after fumbling for a second got his light going again. There was Daddy furiously struggling with a man.

'Up the ladder, Jean,' called Alan, 'and shout for someone to open.'

Then without waiting to see that she did so he rushed to Daddy's aid. The struggle was so violent that it was awkward to know what to do to help, but when he saw that the strange man was pressing Daddy backwards in a dangerous-looking curve he knew that he must do something drastic. Stooping down he caught the man by the ankle and tugged with a sudden jerk. The result was better than he hoped, for the man toppled over with Daddy on top of him, and in falling he hit his head a resounding whack on the stony floor. Alan felt a big torch sticking out of the man's pocket and at once seized it. Instantly he flooded the place with light and saw that Daddy had the man pinned to the ground. One glance showed him that it was Stidson. His eyes were closed and he looked pale by the light of the torch.

Daddy was gasping and panting with his exertions, but Alan said:

'Get up, Daddy; he won't move for a bit. I think he has given his head a nasty wallop. Are you hurt?'

'Not much, my son, but I'm not used to this sort of scrapping. I can stand a punch or two, but I don't like being hugged by a man with arms like he has. You did well to bring him down.'

While they were still looking at him the door above opened and he heard David's voice calling, 'Coo-ee!'

Jean was out in a second, but Daddy called after her.

'Ask Mummy to phone the police. Tell her we have made a capture. Don't frighten her.'

'Mummy's got two policemen with her now,' called David.

'Run and fetch them quickly, then.'

David darted off with Jean after him, and in a very short time Inspector Snelgrove and a very burly sergeant of police came down the ladder. It was with the greatest pleasure that they lifted up the slowly awakening Stidson and hauled him up the ladder. Daddy was the last one to come out and Mummy had arrived to see if there was anything she could do. When she saw Mr Mackie with a cut eye and a bleeding nose, and looking very much the worse for wear, she did not give even one glance at the captive, but bore Daddy off to doctor his wounds.

Alan had to explain to the Inspector what had happened.

'Ah!' he said. 'It was him you saw last night, all right. I had an idea he was still hanging around here. I expect he has been using your secret chamber as his hiding-place. Well, we'll put him in a safe place and then I'll come back and see your father again.'

Stidson was carried off to South Moxton to be locked up. He seemed very dazed, and before he went Mummy bathed his head and stuck some plaster over a nasty gash in his scalp.

The Inspector seemed a bit impatient with Mrs Mackie for taking so much trouble, but she silenced him by saying that she was bound to do it.

'I couldn't send him away in that condition,' she said.

The children were wild with excitement at the turn events had taken.

'What a good job,' said Michael, 'that you had Daddy with you. He would have got away otherwise.'

Daddy grinned, although it hurt his wounded face to do so.

'This is what I get for coming home to have a quiet day with my family. And I have to be in London tomorrow morning to interview some very influential people. I hope they'll like the look of me.'

'How fortunate that the Inspector had chosen this very time to call in,' said Mummy.

'Yes, what brought him here?'

'He came to say that he was certain Stidson was hiding about the place somewhere. He was just asking me if I could show him the priest's hole when David came dashing in yelling for help. He scared me; I could not think what had happened.'

David chuckled. 'You should have seen that fat sergeant squeezing himself down the ladder. His face got redder and redder. And I'm sure I heard two buttons go pop.'

While they were still chattering about it all Jerry came in.

'I say,' he said, as though he were telling them some news, 'I've just seen a car going down the road with two bobbies in it, and they had a very battered-looking fellow with them.'

Then seeing the amused look on all the children's faces, he added: 'Didn't come from here, did he?'

'Come and have a look at my father, then you'll know,' said Alan.

'Your guv'nor? Is he here? I thought he was in America.'

'So did we, but he came home unexpectedly last night.'

'In an aeroplane,' said Elizabeth.

Jerry was presented to Daddy, who was very pleased to meet Alan's friend. After a few polite questions Jerry asked:

'What sort of a plane did you come in, sir?'

'You must forgive me, Jerry, I know it is an unforgivable sin, really, to the modern schoolboy, but I don't know.'

'Don't know!'

'Dreadful as it may seem, I don't. I know it had wings and an engine, and controls and things, and I know I felt a bit sick, but that is all.'

'And do you mean to say that you flew the Atlantic without even knowing the make of plane you were in?'

The children shrieked and Daddy smiled as broadly as the plaster would let him.

'Whatever made you think I flew the Atlantic?'

'Elizabeth said you did.'

'Oo! I didn't. What a whopper!'

'You said . . . '

'I said . . . '

'You misunderstood one another, that's all,' said Daddy. 'Sorry to have spoiled the show, Jerry, but I only flew in a passenger plane from Southampton.'

After that Jerry had little use for Mr Mackie. He was frankly disgusted with anyone who could ride in a plane and know nothing about it except that it had wings, engines, and things.

Later in the day the children and Auntie and Chris and Jerry went off with their tea to a high spot on the moors which gave them a grand view of miles of coast. Mummy wanted them out of the way for she still had much to talk to Daddy about. They were not left to enjoy much peace, though, for the Inspector was back again with Maclean and two other men. He asked to be shown the working of the various doors into and out of the secret places, and then he and his helpers went on with their investigations.

What the results of their search were no one knew for some while. Daddy was told he would have to attend the police court the next morning at ten o'clock to give evidence against Stidson. That he said was impossible, so he then had to go across to the house of the nearest magistrate, who happened to be Colonel Ridler and make a sworn statement.

The Inspector left a warning that Alan would have to go and give evidence of the finding of the boxes and of Stidson's attack on his father.

Mummy was terribly anxious that Micky should not be called, although he himself was just itching to go and tell his story. He was disappointed because the Inspector agreed that unless it was absolutely necessary nothing should be said about his adventure at Spion Kop.

Daddy wanted to see Spion Kop, but had not time.

'As it is,' he said, 'instead of having a day of peaceful enjoyment of the society of my family I seem to have been pushed into the midst of what I have not even seen in America, a sort of gangster film story.'

'Not a bit of it, Daddy,' said Jean. 'There has been nobody shot.'

'Just as well, I should think. My face is painful enough as it is, and how I am going to make myself presentable enough to meet those gentlemen tomorrow I don't know.'

'I know,' said David. 'You'll have to tell them you foolishly allowed your wife to drive the car.'

'Rude child,' said Mummy. 'I've never done anything worse than drive through a wire fence in my life.'

'Did you drive through a wire fence?' asked Jean.

'Yes,' said Daddy, 'and I had to cut a good many strands of Farmer Williams' perfectly new fencing to get the car out, too.'

'Anyway, you might say that your plane crashed,' suggested Micky.

'If you don't mind,' said Daddy, 'I think, if it is necessary to make any explanation at all, I'll tell the truth and say I was attacked by a . . . '

'Do say "gangster", please,' cried Jean.

'I won't. I don't like the word. I'll say a gentleman who wanted to pass out of a doorway at the same moment as I wanted to pass in.'

In the morning Daddy had to start away very early and Mummy had to drive him to the station. The children were all up to give him a cheery send-off. After he had gone Elizabeth made a remark that called down a chorus of protest on her head. She said: 'I wish in a way Daddy had not come.'

Later she explained what she meant. 'Well, it is rotten his going away. We did not expect him for another two months, and were prepared to wait and put up with it, but his coming like that has given us the same feeling as we had when he went away first.'

'But still it is nice to have had him.'

'Yes, but I saw tears in Mummy's eyes this morning, and if he had never come Mummy would not have felt so bad about it.'

'H'm! I think there is something in what you say,' said Alan. 'But what about the joy we all had on Saturday night when we knew he was here? Wasn't that good enough to make up for parting?'

'Yes,' said Jean, 'but the parting comes afterwards, and we remember it longer for that reason.'

When Mummy came back she drove Alan over to the police court. He was not there many minutes for he was not wanted after all. The Inspector asked that the prisoner might be remanded for a week as there would probably be a number of charges against him, and probably there would be further arrests. So that was that, and Alan had nothing to tell the others when he returned.

'Now, my dears, so many things have happened here that we did not expect, that there is a danger of the holiday doing you no good at all. For the rest of the time we are here I want you to promise me that you will not go near the old part of the house unless you all go together to play in your theatre.'

All the Mackies promised, and then Mummy went on. 'For the rest of the time we can have our enjoyment without looking for further adventures.'

'We need not look for them,' said Michael, 'but if they just come we can't help it, can we?'

'No, my son, but I think we have had enough of adventure for one holiday. We'll now look for fun, and I'm sure we'll find it.'

'Shall we be able to go mackerel fishing with Maclean?' asked David.

'Yes, if the weather is good, but I'm taking no risks about anything until we are back home again and you are all safely off to school.'

'Oh! school,' said Jean. 'Don't let's talk about it yet.'

'I love school,' said Elizabeth.

'So does Jean really; she just pretends she doesn't,' replied Mummy.

The meeting then went on to discuss a birthday present for Auntie. When that problem was settled they all went off to prepare fishing lines and spinners in the hope that Maclean would take them out that evening.

CHAPTER XV

Aboard the Yacht

By the time the holiday was drawing to a close and there was talk of returning home, Mrs Mackie and the children had got to know quite a number of people in the neighbourhood. Oxmouth Manor had been empty so long that everyone was pleased to see it occupied once more, and a happy party of children there, too.

One night Mummy was talking about the place to Alan and Jean, and she told them that although they bought the house and land very cheaply it was such an expensive place to run that they had to make some money out of it somehow.

'Oh!' cried Alan, in real alarm, 'you aren't going to sell it again, are you?'

'No, my dear, but during the months when we are not using it ourselves we hope to let it. In that way we shall reduce the cost to ourselves.'

Jean made a face. 'I can't bear the thought,' she said, 'of strangers coming here and living in our place. Suppose they make a muck of it.'

'Of course we should be careful to find out the sort of people we were letting it to, and I don't like the idea any more than you do, especially now that we have settled into it and become so attached to everything about it.'

'Don't think I'm trying to be horrid, Mummy,' said Alan, 'but I sincerely hope you will not be able to let it.'

'I know how you feel, Alan, but it is costing more than we anticipated, and if we are to keep it for a holiday home for ourselves we shall be bound to let it for part of the year.'

'If that's the case,' said Jean, 'I hope some rich man will come along soon and pay us a lot of money for the time he has it.'

Mrs Mackie's answer was so unexpected that they both looked at her wonderingly. She said:

'Have you looked out in the bay this evening?'

'Not to notice anything particularly. Why?'

'Come with me,' said Mummy.

They followed her out through the garden, down the little tunnel, and so out on to the cliff.

'Look!' she said.

'A ship!' they both cried. 'I've never seen one so close into our bay as that before. Doesn't she look lovely with all those lights reflected in the sea!'

'What is she?' asked Jean. 'A pleasure cruiser?'

'She isn't big enough for a cruising liner, is she, Mummy?'

'She is not a liner, but she is a pleasure ship. She is a private yacht belonging to a very rich gentleman Daddy met in America.'

'I think I'm beginning to understand,' said Alan.

'What?' asked Jean.

'The connexion between what Mummy has just been talking about and the presence of this lovely ship.'

'Do you mean . . . ?'

'Yes,' said Mummy. 'On board that ship is a gentleman by the perfectly thrilling name of Hiram P. Soss. He has made heaps of money out of . . .'

'H.P. Sauce,' interrupted Alan.

'No, out of patent pills, potions, and powders. Daddy says he is one of the most charming men he has ever met in his life. He is coming ashore here in the morning to see us and our house. If he likes it he is going to take it for six months at least, and he will pay us well for it.'

'Then I hope he likes it.'

'Yes, because if he does it will make certain that we shall be able to come here again next year.'

'At the same time, I hate the thought of strangers using our house.'

'Yes, but even more I should hate the thought of not being able to have it when we wanted it next summer.'

The next morning the Mackies were on the beach having one of their usual games of tap and run after their swim, casting occasional glances to the vessel riding so gracefully at anchor about a mile out, when there was a cry from Mummy.

'Look! there is a boat coming from the ship. I expect that is Mr Soss coming ashore to see me. He promised to come this morning.'

The game was stopped to watch the progress of the boat. It seemed a very long time in reaching the shore, but at last it was carefully nosed into the sand and the children rushed into the water to help drag it in. Mummy was only a little way behind, waiting to receive her guest.

Before they were able to lay hands on it the Mackies had taken stock of the boat and its occupants. Everything about it and them was very smart and clean-looking.

'Our boat doesn't look like that,' said Micky.

'We aren't millionaires,' replied Jean.

The boat was manned by a crew of three; two men at the oars and one at the tiller. Mr Soss sat very upright amidships as though he hardly liked trusting himself to such a small craft.

'I don't wonder,' whispered David, 'seeing the size of him.'

Mr Soss was indeed a big man, in fact, huge; and his bulk only became apparent when he stood up to step ashore. He was literally a man-mountain; not fat, but just an enormous man, built on battleship lines, as Alan afterwards remarked.

He greeted the children in a voice that did credit to his great chest; he positively roared at them as he leapt with astonishing nimbleness from his little boat to the shore.

'Well, kids,' he cried. 'Here comes the American invader leaping ashore like Julius Caesar.'

'Much more like some great Viking chief,' said Alan.

The remark seemed to please him, for he laughed aloud and strode forward, sweeping his hat from his head to greet Mrs Mackie.

'Mrs Mackenzie?' he said. 'I'm Soss, Hiram P. Soss. There is no one here to make the introductions so I must do it myself.'

'How do you do?' said Mummy. 'My husband told me to expect you.'

'Yes, he told me all about you and those wonderful kids of yours. My! but they're cute. Now, you'll forgive me for seeming abrupt, but if you'll allow me I would like to do my business first. I'm just crazy to know these youngsters better, but I never allow pleasure to stand before business.'

Mummy smiled. 'Come along, then,' she said, 'we will go up to the house, and then we can come back here afterwards.'

They went away in close conversation, and the children turned their attention to the American sailors. They asked thousands of questions about everything they could think of, from New York sky-scrapers to Hollywood, from the Mississippi to Seattle, from the Grand Canyon to Chicago hold-ups, but never once was there a personal question about Mr Soss or his business.

The sailors enjoyed themselves as much as the children did, and asked a good many questions in return. They hauled the boat well above the tide and gave a lesson in the art of baseball playing. One of them hit the ball so far that the Mackies were quite staggered and made a hero of him at once. When they heard that he really had been a famous player in his time they wanted to see more of his prowess.

At last Mummy and Mr Soss were seen coming down the cliff again. Mummy was smiling happily and Mr Soss was smoking a very long cigar, and really expanding with obvious pleasure.

When he came near he called to the children, and they deserted the baseball player for the company of this splendid-looking man.

'Hey!' he cried. 'I just want to know you kids. Come and talk to Hiram.'

He sat down on the sand and they gathered round him. He inquired the name and age of each one, and asked ever so many questions. He set them all at ease and they talked to him very freely. At last Mummy thought it was time to interrupt.

'Mr Soss will be tired of all your chatter.'

'No, ma'am,' he said. 'I could listen to these kids of yours for hours. They're just too cute. I'm tickled to death with their speech. It is lovely to hear the English language spoken by well-brought-up English children. My friends in America have said to me many times, "If you want to hear English spoken as it ought to be you must get into a family where kids will talk. Decently educated English children speak perfectly!" '

'Mummy doesn't always think so,' said Michael. 'She says I'm always using the wrong words.'

'That's not what I mean. I don't care how many wrong words you use, it is the *sound* of your speech that thrills me. Now I have two boys, they're much older than you, but they never spoke like you do.'

Mrs Mackie tried to turn the conversation. 'Mr Soss likes our house very much.'

'I sure do,' he replied, 'but your mother is a good business woman.'

'Did she stick you up for a big rent?' asked Alan.

Mummy looked vexed at this remark, but Hiram roared aloud.

'No,' he said, 'she didn't do any sticking up, but she gave me some Bristol milk.'

'Oo!' said Elizabeth quietly to Micky. 'Isn't Mummy going red in the face?'

'What's Bristol milk?' asked Jean.

'I know,' said Alan.

Mr Soss laughed again. 'That Bristol cow must be some animal,' he said.

Mummy was by this time so confused that she did not know what to do. 'I didn't give it you to try to . . . ' she began.

'Pardon me ma'am; when I said you were a good business woman I meant it. We have struck a bargain that satisfies us both, and if that marvellous Bristol cow has helped to do it I'm sure delighted.'

All the children, except Alan, were quite puzzled over this matter of the Bristol cow, but their attention was distracted by Mr Soss saying:

'Now I'm going to have a nice little party on board my vessel this afternoon, and I want you all to come to it; all of you.'

Everybody was effusive with thanks, but he cut them short.

'I'm a greedy old man,' he said, 'and I'm doing it for my pleasure, not yours.'

'I don't believe that,' said Elizabeth. 'I think you want to give us a treat.'

'I want to give myself one, little sweetheart.'

'It will be a treat for us, anyway,' said David.

'Right! I'll send a boat ashore for you at four o'clock. Good-bye.'

They launched his boat with a will and gave a resounding cheer as he rowed away, waving and waving until they were tired.

All the way home the children could talk of nothing but the promised visit to the yacht, but Alan drew back with Mrs Mackie to talk to her quietly.

'Satisfied, Mummy?'

'More than satisfied, my son. Mr Soss was teasing me when he said I was a good business woman. I asked him a very big rent for the place, thinking he would want to bargain and beat me down, but he just snapped at it. He is taking the place for six months with the option of taking it again next year.'

'So that means . . .'

'It means that we are safe for our holidays here for the next two summers, and if for any reason we had to sell the place Mr Soss would buy it, I'm sure.'

'I hope that will never come.'

'So do I.'

Four o'clock found the whole tribe of Mackies, including Chris, clambering into the big boat that Mr Soss had sent to fetch them. Their baseball friend of the morning was in charge, and he treated them, 'just as though we were all admirals,' said Micky.

The journey to the yacht was somewhat choppy, and Auntie and Mummy were both looking a delicate shade of green by the time they were put aboard, but they soon recovered themselves on the steadier vessel, although they could not enjoy themselves quite as they would for thinking of the return journey. The children were not affected by any qualms and gave themselves up to unqualified enjoyment.

The ship was called *Margaret Soss*. Michael wanted to ask why, but didn't quite like to. One of the sailors explained that she was called after Mr Soss's wife who had died several years before.

Certainly she was a thing of great beauty. The Mackies were openly amazed and thrilled by all they saw. Mr Soss himself conducted them round the ship and showed them all its wonders.

'What gorgeous cabins!' cried Jean.

'How clean and polished everything is,' said David.

'What topping engines she has,' remarked Elizabeth.

They all had plenty of comments to make, and were almost beyond further thrills when they were called to tea by a uniformed boy with a bugle. Michael could hardly restrain himself from asking if he might have a blow at that bugle.

To Mr Soss he said: 'What a lucky boy that is!'

'Why, kiddie?'

'He wears such a lovely uniform and he has a bugle to blow.'

Mummy said: 'I think that is the height of Michael's ambition at present, to wear a uniform and blow a bugle.'

'Yes,' said Micky, 'but on a ship, too.'

Tea was a marvellous affair. The children were almost silent from wonderment at how such dainties could be produced on board ship, but that did not prevent them from clearing the decks of the fare put before them. Mummy and Auntie were both seriously alarmed at the number of ices consumed, but Mr Soss declared that they were the finest food in the world.

After tea they played a number of deck games, and then Mummy said she thought they had overstayed their welcome.

'No,' said Mr Soss, 'I have not enjoyed myself as much as this for years. I want to give your kids one more treat.'

'What's that?' they all cried.

'You shall go for a little cruise in my ship, and you shall all stand upon the bridge like officers and see the handling of the vessel.'

'Please,' said David, 'I would rather go into the engine-room and stand by the engineer and see what happens.'

'So you shall then.'

Mr Soss sent his compliments to the captain and asked that the children might be entertained in this particular manner.

They saw the hauling up of the anchor, also the working of the telegraph to the engine-room. Then they started in a wide sweep out to sea, passing round the point towards Morley Bay. They did about an hour's cruise, and then as the light was beginning to fail and the captain wanted to be in a safe anchorage before dark they came back to almost the identical spot from which they started. They were put in the boat again and, amid a chorus of thanks and farewells, were rowed home.

Edna greeted them with a message.

'Someone rang up for you, ma'am,' she said. 'A gentleman from Exeter.'

'From Exeter? Who was he?'

'He would not give his name, but said he was the secretary of some society or other; I could not make out the name. He is going to ring up again presently.'

'Somebody begging for help for some organization or other, I expect,' said Auntie.

'Those sort of people usually write, don't they, Mummy?'

'Yes, Jean, they do; but there is no knowing what people will do to rook you of money in these days. Well, if he is going to ring up again I shall know who he is.'

Within a very few minutes the expected call came. Mrs Mackie herself answered the phone.

'Yes?'

'Is that Mrs Mackenzie?'

'Yes.'

'My name is Peterson. I am the secretary of the South-Western Counties Society of Antiquaries.'

'Yes?'

'Mr Mackenzie has told me in a letter that I might apply to you for permission to see over your house. I am compiling a book on the old houses of your district with a special chapter dealing with secret chambers, priests' holes, and the like.'

There was a very deep frown on Mummy's face and the children wondered why, but, of course, they could not hear anything but her side of the conversation which, so far, had been limited to one word.

'When do you want to come?'

'As soon as possible if you don't mind. I am going to Germany lecturing very shortly and I want to get my book as far forward as possible before I go. Could I come tomorrow morning?'

'Well, I suppose so, although it is not a very convenient time.'

'I do not want to put you out. Would the afternoon suit you better?'

'No, if you are coming tomorrow at all the morning will perhaps suit me better.'

'Thank you very much. I am most grateful to you. I will be there about eleven. Thank you. Good-bye.'

'Good-bye.'

Mummy rang off with a puzzled look in her eyes. The children wondered, but asked no questions. Mummy told them nothing, but beckoned to Auntie and they had a private conversation for a few minutes.

While Auntie was seeing to the bathing and bedding of a very happy family of young children, thoroughly delighted with their outing, Mummy called Alan and said:

'I am going to pay a call. I would like you to come with me.'

'Can I come, too?' asked Jean.

'Not this time, sweetheart.'

Alan asked no questions, but accompanied his mother in the car to the house of Colonel Ridler. They found the gentleman at home, and he was full of courtesy and eagerness to know if he could be of any service.

'You are an antiquary and archaeologist, aren't you?' began Mrs Mackie.

'Yes, in a very humble kind of way.'

'Well, is there a society known as the South-Western Counties Society of Antiquaries?'

'There may be, but I've never heard of it.'

'Do you know, or know of, a man named Peterson, who is supposed to be the secretary of this society?'

'No, I think not. I imagine I know all the best-known archaeologists of this part of the world, too.'

'I was suspicious.'

'Suspicious of what?'

'I have had a phone message from a man who calls himself Peterson tonight, saying my husband has given him permission to explore our house and asking me to fix a suitable time.'

'You haven't done it?'

'Yes, I have. He is coming tomorrow morning.'

'I shouldn't admit him.'

'Well, after all, he may be genuine, and I should not like to insult anyone to whom my husband had offered this courtesy.'

'But you say you are suspicious.'

'Yes.'

'Of what?'

'I don't know, quite. In some vague way the man's voice seemed familiar, though I can't quite place it. I could almost swear I have spoken to him before.'

'What do you intend to do?'

'I wondered if you could manage to come round tomorrow morning to meet him? I could introduce you as a friend who is very interested in the subject of old houses.'

'Certainly I'll come. What time?'

'Before eleven. He is supposed to be coming at eleven.'

'I'll be there, and if he is one of the regular attendants at our antiquarian excursions I shall recognize him for certain.'

After Mrs Mackie had expressed her thanks she and Alan started for home again.

'What's in the wind, now, Mummy?' asked Alan.

'Maybe nothing, my child, except that your mother is making a silly of herself. Yet I don't think so.'

'Neither do I. It isn't our old friend Simpson by any chance, is it?'

'Ah!' cried Mummy. 'Simpson, Donaldson, Peterson.

Your criminal is seldom a man of much imagination. It may be the same man, whose powers of invention, where names are concerned, does not run beyond names ending in -son.'

'If it is, what can he want?'

'That is for us to find out, I think we'll have a word with Inspector Snelgrove on our way home.'

They found the Inspector in his office, and told him the whole story.

'I'll be prepared,' he said. 'The man may be, as you say, perfectly straight, but if he is the person I think he is I'll have a nice little trap laid for him. I'll be round early in the morning to make my own plans. You'll keep this a secret, won't you?'

'Certainly I will. Good night.'

When they were once more in the car Alan said:

'I believe we are going to end our holiday with some more excitement.'

'Perhaps,' said Mrs Mackie. 'Then you will have to come down to earth with a bump, for next week it will be home again and then school.'

'Home again? This is home, too, isn't it?'

'Yes, I suppose it is. We have had a good time, haven't we?'

'Mummy, it has been heavenly, and I think it ought to send us all back to school again to work like Britons.'

'I hope that feeling will last, my son.'

'It will. You'll see. But I can't help wondering if tomorrow is going to give us more excitement as a sort of final kick, as Mr Soss would say. You know, Mummy, he made me laugh today. He said such a funny thing. I told him I hoped to go to America one day and perhaps I should call to see him. What d'you think he said?'

'Something American, I expect.'

'He said, "Oh! Boy! If you do I'll kick two chairs over."'

That night Alan could not get to sleep for a long time, wondering what the next morning was going to bring in the way of a last adventure.

CHAPTER XVI

David Plays Trumps

ALAN was about very early the next morning, and to the surprise of the whole family, so was Mummy. She had a feeling of excitement which she tried hard not to communicate to the children, but she did not succeed very well. As soon as breakfast was over, she said:

'Now I want you children out of the way this morning. I am expecting some visitors, so you can have lunch packed and go off for the day. I have told Cook what to prepare for you and you can have the day to yourselves. All I stipulate is that you don't do anything that you know very well I should not allow if you were with me.'

'Can we fish off the rocks at the far end of the beach?' asked Jean.

'You can do anything sensible.'

Alan followed his mother from the room. 'Must I go with them?' he asked.

'Yes, dear.'

'I wanted to be in the fun, if there is going to be any.'

'There may be nothing doing, and if there is it would be better for you to be out of it.'

'But I'm sure Daddy would say I ought to have stayed by you.'

'Daddy would say what he always says. "Do what Mummy tells you." '

Alan was not pleased and not too happy, either, but Mummy restored his good humour by saying, 'Besides, I don't like the idea of the others being alone all day without you to keep an eye on them.'

So he went off to get ready with the rest of the family.

At nine o'clock Mr Snelgrove came to the back door. He was not in uniform and had sneaked in by climbing over the wall from the lane behind the cow-shed. He explained that he did not come in openly in case anyone was watching the house.

'I don't think I was spotted,' he said. 'In a few minutes a man will come here selling laces and buttons and such-like oddments. He is one of my men and I want you to admit him. I have two more men hiding among the rocks below your cave. I sent them round by boat. Now I think we are prepared for all comers. I want you to let me down into the secret tunnel. I'll wait some distance down, but I shall be on the alert to come if I am wanted.'

Colonel Ridler arrived soon after ten. He blew in with a gust of cheerfulness. He greeted Mrs Mackie with a hearty laugh.

'Do you know,' he said, 'I shall be downright disappointed if this man turns out to be genuine. I'm really looking forward to a bit of fun. A scrap would do me good. Where are the children?'

'Down on the beach. I thought it wiser to get them out of the way.'

'Much wiser. Now what are we going to do?'

There was a council of war between the colonel, the Inspector, and Mrs Mackie, and all their plans were carefully laid. When they had finished the Inspector laughed.

'We shall look a pack of fools,' he said, 'if this man turns out to be a genuine harmless archaeologist.'

'We have to risk that,' said Mummy.

It was exactly eleven o'clock when the front-door bell rang with a loud peal. Edna opened the door and showed the visitor into the drawing-room. She then came and told Mrs Mackie.

'Mr Peterson has called.'

'Thank you, Edna,' said Mummy. Then turning to the colonel she added, 'Now for it.'

As she entered the drawing-room Mrs Mackie had quite a shock. She was quite prepared to see someone bearing at any rate some resemblance to the man they had met at the fair but this man was as unlike him as could possibly be.

The man Donaldson, or Simpson, had been a man of

slight build but very upright carriage; a man who might reasonably be described as 'dapper'. This man who rose to greet her with a very polite bow was extremely old and bent. He had heavy round shoulders, which looked even more massive owing to the nature of the big coat he wore. It was very old-fashioned, and had a large Inverness cape to it. He had a reddish beard, and he wore spectacles with very thick lenses. He poked his head and peered at Mrs Mackie as he spoke to her.

'It is extremely good of you to receive me, especially at such short notice,' he said. 'I met your husband on board ship coming home from America, not long ago, and he told me a great deal about this house.'

'Do sit down,' interrupted Mummy.

'Thank you. He very kindly promised me that I should visit him here next time he was in England, but he explained that his visit was too short to allow of it.'

'Quite right; he was only here for one day; he had just come over for an important business conference.'

'Yes, so I gathered. He left me his address in New York, and I took the liberty of writing to him and he very kindly replied by return suggesting that I should put myself in communication with you.'

Mrs Mackie was completely satisfied with this story, and was already blaming herself for having been so suspicious and for having dragged Colonel Ridler and Inspector Snelgrove out on a fool's errand.

'Will you excuse me a minute,' she said. 'I would like you to take a glass of wine before we start on a round of the house.'

'Please don't trouble, Mrs Mackenzie.'

'No trouble at all; I'll be back in a moment.'

As soon as Mrs Mackie had carefully closed the door she darted into the next room to speak to the Colonel.

'Sold,' she said. 'Nothing like the man. He's quite genuine. He met my husband on the boat. Come in and be introduced.'

'Never mind,' replied the Colonel. 'No harm ever comes of being well prepared.'

Mrs Mackie signalled to Edna to bring in refreshment, and she took the colonel in to be introduced to her visitor.

'Mr Peterson, may I introduce Colonel Ridler, a neighbour who is also a keen antiquary. He is so interested in the subject of your forthcoming book that I am sure you will have much in common.'

Mr Peterson did not seem at all pleased to meet the gallant colonel, and had very little to say to him at first. That did not prevent the colonel from asking a number of questions, to which he returned somewhat vague answers. After a very few minutes the visitor asked if he might now be taken over the house, especially the old part, as his time was short.

'Of course,' said Mrs Mackie. 'I know you will excuse me, but Colonel Ridler knows his way about the house quite well, and he will act as your guide. We are preparing to return to Town shortly and I have much to see to.'

'Thank you, thank you. I am very much obliged. Shall we start?'

As they moved out into the hall Mrs Mackie was surprised and vexed to see David just coming down the stairs.

'I thought you were on the beach, David,' she said.

'I only came back for something,' replied David. 'I'm sorry, Mummy.'

He was about to slip out of the door when Mr Peterson spoke to him.

'Is this your son? How like his father he is!'

David gazed at him as though he were some strange monster from a museum, and the two gentlemen passed on.

'Mummy!' whispered David.

'Go along, boy. You have no business here. I can't stop to talk to you.'

'But Mummy,' he insisted, 'who is that man?'

'A friend of Daddy's. Go back to the beach at once.'

'But, Mummy . . .'

'Either go out or go to your bed.'

'I only wanted to say that the man with a beard has a

crooked finger on his left hand exactly like that Mr Simpson we met at the fair.'

'What!' Mummy almost screamed it at him.

'Yes. It's the little finger. You see when he comes back.'

'Are you sure of that?'

'Positive. Besides, that reddy-coloured hair of his is a wig.'

'What makes you say that?'

'When I was coming down the stairs I was looking down on him and I'm sure it's a wig.'

'Now, my son,' said Mummy, 'you have the chance of your life to show what you are made of. Hurry down to the beach and take Jean with you and go to the cave. Say nothing to Jean in front of the others.'

'Why not Alan?'

'I want Alan to take care of Micky and Elizabeth. You are to take Jean with you; climb into the cave as soon as you can. Run up the tunnel, and in there somewhere you will find Inspector Snelgrove. Tell him that Colonel Ridler will be bringing the gentleman down, and then tell him what you have just told me.'

'About the wig and the crooked finger?'

'Yes, then as soon as you have told him come away at once. If he wants you to take a message or anything you must do it.'

'There are two policemen down there hiding among the rocks; I saw them but they didn't see me.'

'Run on, now, and don't waste a second.'

'Just a tick; I must get a torch.'

In two minutes David was off as fast as he could run. He hurled himself down over the cliff to the beach, he was in such a hurry. He did not stop to consider the risk of a broken leg. He found Jean by herself and told her what Mummy had said. She scented adventure and they hastily ran to Alan and told him they had a job to do for Mummy.

'What?' he asked.

'Tell you when we come back.'

Just as they commenced to climb the rocks to the cave

one of the hiding policemen pounced out on them and cried:

'Now then, where are you off to?'

'We have to go to the cave,' said David.

'No you don't. You just stay down.'

'But Mummy sent us,' said Jean.

'I can't help that. I've orders that anybody I find making for that cave is to be stopped and held till the Inspector orders otherwise.'

'Yes, but . . . ' began David.

'No buts about it, sonny.'

'This is our private beach,' said Jean, indignantly, 'and we have a perfect right to climb up into our own cave.'

'I'm not talking about rights and wrongs; I'm talking about my orders, so just you go back to your play.'

'Very well,' said David. 'If you get into a row I can't help it. I've been sent with a message to Inspector Snelgrove, who is up in the tunnel, and if he does not get the message he may be killed, so where will you and your orders be, then?'

The bobby hesitated at this. At last he said:

'Tunnel? What tunnel?'

'There's a tunnel up there, leading to our house,' said Jean.

'Wait a minute,' he said, and then he called, 'Charlie!'

'Hullo!' came a voice from a little distance away.

'Come here a minute.'

Another policeman appeared and David had to tell his story over again. Then there were more questions until at last Jean became very impatient and said:

'If you waste any more time we shall be too late with our warning. You have kept us hanging about a long time as it is.'

At last the one named Charlie said:

'I know. I'll go up with them, and if there is really a tunnel there I shall know that they are speaking the truth, and I'll let 'em go.'

'Truth!' said Jean, scornfully. 'What do you think we want to tell untruths for? This is important.'

Accompanied by Charlie they climbed up. He could not go

as quickly as they could and expressed astonishment at the ease with which they picked out a way.

'We have been up scores of times,' said David. 'It was a bit dangerous until we found the best path.'

'Never knew there was a cave up there until this morning.'

'That shows,' said Jean, 'that you have never been in the smuggling business around here.'

'Smuggling, eh?'

'Yes. There's plenty of it goes on, and this cave is the principal place in it.'

'Really, you surprise me.'

Presently they were in the cave, and the man was quite prepared to find that there was no such thing as a tunnel, but did not offer to apologize when he found there was.

David took out his torch and closely followed by Jean dashed off up the rocky way. They did not stop to consider anything except that they had a highly important message to deliver quickly. They did not reckon how far they had gone, but went blundering forward until a harsh voice startled them with a loud cry of, 'Stand there!'

They both stopped short, panting.

'My word! What a fright that gave me!' said Jean.

'Is that Inspector Snelgrove?' asked David.

'Well, what about it?' asked the officer, coming a pace or two down the tunnel and passing a brilliant beam over them.

'Please, sir,' said David, 'Mummy has sent us with a message. There is a gentleman coming down here with Colonel Ridler.'

'Well, what about him?'

'I'm not altogether sure, but I know he is not the man the colonel thinks he is.'

'How do you know that?'

'I recognized just one little thing about him. He has a crooked little finger on his left hand.'

'What! Are you sure?'

'Positive.'

'Smart of you to see that.'

'Yes, I am an observant child,' said David, without the slightest sign of a smile.

'Well, my dears, the best thing you can do is to get out of here quickly and find one of my men and send him to me.'

'Shall we send Charlie?'

'Either of them. Hurry now, and get right away. I don't want you children about when Simpson – Donaldson – Peterson appears. From your remark about the crooked little finger I guess I know who he is, and he is not a pleasant gentleman to tackle in a narrow passage. Be off, now.'

They turned about, and David could not resist a temptation to have a dig at the Inspector.

'It has been no trouble to us at all,' he said.

Snelgrove laughed. 'Thank you,' he said. 'I'm sorry I forgot my manners. I shall not forget you, though.'

'Cheerio!' cried David, and back they went to find Charlie. Much to their annoyance they couldn't find him.

'He must have climbed down again,' said Jean.

'Then he will have the pleasure of climbing up again,' laughed David. 'It will get some of his tummy down a bit.'

Down they went, calling all the way, but there was no sign of Charlie or the other policeman. As they were clambering over a ledge of rock David said:

'Doesn't the *Margaret Soss* look lovely from here?'

'Yes,' replied Jean, 'I suppose she will be sailing soon.'

'Two o'clock this afternoon, the captain told me yesterday. I wish I could go a long voyage in her. Oh, look! There is a motor boat, looks a bit like a racer, coming round the headland. I wonder what she can be coming round so close in for.'

'It's a funny thing we can't find those two policemen,' said David.

'There they are,' said Jean. 'Look, they are having a quiet rest. I expect they are tired of doing nothing.'

'Watch me,' said David. 'I'm going to make them jump.'

He wriggled his way over the rocks so that he could not be seen, and came close behind the two men. Then he shouted as loud as he could, 'Hi!'

Both men jumped up.

'Fine sleuths you are,' said David.

'You young demon!' said one of them.

'The Inspector wants one of you up the tunnel at once; he is expecting a heavy bombardment at any minute.'

'You don't fool me any more,' said Charlie. 'If the Inspector wants to issue any different orders from those he has given already he'll do it himself.'

'Would he? And leave his post to do it, I suppose?'

'Run away and play, my son, and keep to the other end of the beach.'

'You are not going?'

'Certainly not.'

'H'm! I've read in books about people who can obey orders but can't use their brains.'

This made Charlie angry and he rose in his wrath. He made a grab at David and gripped his arm until he squealed.

'You just get out of this,' he said, 'or I'll report you to the Inspector for making uncomplimentary remarks about the officers of the law.'

'Rubbish!' said David, who was both hurt and angry, as well as being worried.

He gave a sharp twist and wrenched his arm away from the policeman's hold and jumped away from rock to rock. To Jean he called:

'Get away down to Alan quickly and stay there. I must go back to the Inspector.'

Charlie heard him and called out: 'Wait a minute!'

'No fear,' shouted David. 'I'm going to tell him the fools he has to deal with.'

He scrambled back yet once again to the cave, and then remembered he had given Jean the torch to hold while he crept over the rocks to the policemen.

'Can't be helped,' he said to himself, 'I must go up without it.' And he started up the tunnel in the dark.

Meanwhile Jean made her way back to Alan and the other two children. Micky and Elizabeth were surf-riding on their boards, and Alan was trying to make cucks and drakes with flat bits of stone over the water.

'What's been going on?' he asked Jean, when she arrived.

Jean sat down with him on the warm sand and told him all that had taken place. Alan looked at the torch in Jean's hand, and said:

'Has he gone up in the dark?'

'Heavens! I forgot to give him the torch.'

'He must be a plucky kid. I don't quite like the idea of him doing it, though. Give me the torch: I'll go after him. You stay with Liz and Mick.'

He jumped up and ran off, but he had not climbed very far before he was seized by Charlie and his mate.

'No you don't,' said one of them. 'There has been too much running up and down here this morning, and we had orders to let nobody go; nobody, do you understand?'

'I hear,' said Alan, and pleaded with them to let him go to his brother's help. They would not listen to him but made him sit down between them.

'You can wait here until he comes down.'

Fuming with annoyance and eagerness to be off Alan sat there, a prisoner. At last he said:

'I suppose you can hear that motor-boat chuffing in the bay.'

'That's nothing. There's plenty of them about.'

'Yes, but that one is close inshore. I don't know what it can be doing, because we don't allow passengers to land here.'

'Go and have a squint, Charlie,' said his mate. So Charlie went. He was soon back and whispered:

'It's a fast boat, by the look of it, and it is close in to the shore just below here. There is only one man in it and he is keeping his engine gently running.'

'Why not go down to investigate?' said Alan.

'No, my son, you don't seem to understand. Our orders is watch, and watch we will. If we stay where we are we can see anybody going up, or coming down without being seen ourselves.'

They sat still a few more minutes, and then they all

heard a sound as of falling stone near them. Charlie stood up.

'Come, Fred,' he shouted. 'There's a bloke running down behind there.'

As he called he leapt forward, and in doing so collapsed with a twisted ankle. 'Go on,' he yelled to Fred. 'After him.'

Alan scrambled on to a high point of rock where he could see the chase, but the stranger was already well away from his pursuer and racing over the sands towards the motor-boat. Alan could see the man was bound to escape and was furious with vexation.

What could he do, he wondered, and as he puzzled for some way to be of use he looked out to the *Margaret Soss* and saw a speck of light.

'Somebody looking this way with a telescope,' he said.

Quick as thought he tore off his coat. Fortunately he had on a white shirt. He stood upright and started to semaphore, STOP THAT BOAT. STOP THAT BOAT. STOP THAT BOAT.

He kept on until his arms ached.

CHAPTER XVII

A Thrilling Chase

Mrs Mackie had instructed Colonel Ridler in the method of gaining access to the priest's hole, and after he had shown most of the old part of the Manor to the visitor he took him to the room with the window-seat. He showed him the manner of opening, and when the old man peered down the hole, he said:

'Dear me, dear me! I should very much like to go down, but I am almost afraid to venture.'

'Why?' asked the colonel, who was rather fed up with the man and tired of his continual chatter.

'Well, you see, I am not so nimble as I was twenty years ago, and I hardly know how to essay that ladder.'

'Quite safe. I'll go first and show you the best way to get down.'

'Thank you, thank you.'

Colonel Ridler let himself down through the hole, and when he had reached the bottom of the ladder he called out:

'Come along. The ladder is quite strong and safe.'

Had the colonel seen what his strange companion was doing at that moment he would have been more on his guard than he was, for the old man moved very quickly to the window and opened and shut it twice.

'I'm coming,' he called, and with great deliberation descended.

'Dear me, dear me' he kept on saying. 'This is really remarkable; a genuine priest's hole. A very fine example, too. About the best I have ever seen. Dear me, dear me! Such unusual mural decoration, too.'

'Yes, but this is not all; if you'll wait a moment while I climb the ladder and close the trap over our heads you will see something else.'

'Dear me. Dear me!'

The colonel sprang up the ladder, and just as he was

balancing himself to get the flap closed over his head the ladder was jerked from under him and he fell to the ground with a crash.

'Dear me, dear me! How very clumsy of me. I caught my foot in the ladder. I do hope you aren't hurt.'

There was no answer from the colonel, and the man stooped over him and examined him by the light of a torch which he hastily drew from his pocket. Apparently quite satisfied he went to the open door and entered the tunnel. When he had passed out he closed the door behind him. It moved quite easily in a way that the Mackies had never been able to make it.

Silently and swiftly he wriggled through the tiny passage behind the door and dragged out the box that Alan had seen there. Quickly he opened it, making a hissing noise between his teeth when he found that it had already been burst open. With eager and trembling hands he tore out the inner lining and gently removed the glass tubes.

'Ah!' he muttered, 'they did not find those.' He very carefully wrapped each one up separately in the cotton-wool packing from the bottom of the box and disposed them about himself in various pockets.

Giving a little chuckle, he squirmed his way out into the tunnel and turned as though to make for the sea. After a second he paused, having heard a slight sound. It was Snelgrove moving cautiously towards him, although he did not know that. However, he guessed that somebody was there and turned to go back the other way. Again the door moved at his touch and he entered the priest's hole once more.

As he did so he encountered an infuriated colonel who had only been temporarily stunned by his fall, but before the attack could be brought home he once again retreated and slammed the door on his assailant's face. The roar of rage that the colonel gave was heard by Snelgrove, who was only a few yards down the tunnel by now.

At once the man threw off the heavy cloak he had been

wearing, removed the thick glasses, and drew back into the little side passage again. Snelgrove came on with his light shining this way and that, but before he turned the corner his enemy was in hiding. He came up to the closed door and he could hear faintly the hammering and raving of the colonel inside.

He put his mouth close to the door and yelled.

'Is that you, Colonel? What's wrong. Can't you let me in?'

The Colonel was making so much noise that he did not hear him, and then Snelgrove was suddenly smothered by a heavy cloak thrown over his head, his torch was snatched from him while he was struggling to free himself, and then he had a severe crack on the back of the head and collapsed in a heap on the floor.

His attacker ran down the tunnel with the certainty of a man who had been down there many times before. He only gave an occasional flash from his light to show him the way.

Meanwhile, David was hurrying up as best as he could in the dark. He saw the light and called out, 'Inspector Snelgrove, I told your men and they won't come because . . .'

He did not get any farther. He felt himself gripped by two powerful hands and he was given a shake which took most of the breath out of his body. No word was said, but he was forced to run with his captor until they reached the cave. Out in the daylight he recognized the man who had captured him. His wig had come off, his glasses were gone, as was the cloak.

'Mr Simpson,' said David.

'You are too smart for a youngster,' the man said. 'You ought to stick to bees and things like that. I can't stop to talk to you, and if you make a noise I'll strangle you. Come on.'

David could see he had a desperate man to deal with, and thought it wiser to do as he was told. He was dragged across the cave, over the heap of rocks behind which he had hidden the morning he had tried to frighten the rest of the family, up to the tiny entrance into a further cave that Alan had spotted on that same morning but had since forgotten all about.

David was thrust through first and the man crawled in after him. It was terribly dark there, but a fresh flash from the torch showed that it was a bigger cave than the outside one. It had evidently been used, for there were boxes and all kinds of litter lying about. Still holding tight to David the man Simpson, for that was his real name, searched about until he found a piece of rope. In two minutes he had David tied up so that he could not move. Then he went off and left him in the darkness.

Silently he crept down the cliff. He could hear the voices of Alan and the two policemen and he was able to avoid them. He could also hear the sound of the boat which he knew was waiting to rush him out to sea and safety. As bad luck would have it he kicked over a piece of loose rock and he was heard.

When he saw that he was being chased he did not attempt to hide himself, but raced for the beach and the boat. He reached it in safety and threw himself into it.

'Let her go,' he cried.

Instantly she roared into life and sped for the open sea.

'Did you get them?' inquired the steersman.

'Of course I did,' Simpson snapped. 'Don't talk; make her fly. What's that boat out there?'

'Only an American yacht; we've nothing to fear from her.'

'Open her out, man, open her out. Speed, speed!'

'We can't do any more than this. We shall bust the engine if we force her too far.'

Almost leaping bodily out of the waves the racing-boat rushed on. Simpson had an eye only for the shore to see if any pursuers had spotted his method of escape. His eye was caught by a white figure perched half-way up the cliff.

'Here,' he cried to the man at the wheel, 'can you look astern a second?'

'What is it?'

'It looks to me like somebody signalling.'

The man gave a quick glance ashore. 'That's it,' he said, 'somebody is signalling, but I can't think who he is signalling to.'

'Perhaps the American. We needn't fear him. He can't stop us. Go right ahead.'

Rapidly they were approaching the *Margaret Soss*, intending to pass within half a mile of her. Suddenly they heard another roar above the sound of their own engine, and from behind the American ship there came a mighty speed-boat. It was a giant racer, and the two men knew at once that they had no hope of escape if the other was chasing them.

Simpson tried to stand up so that he might see better.

'There are five men in her,' he said, 'and two are in uniform.'

They put their helm a little to starboard to try to shoot between the on-coming boat and the headland, but in less than a quarter of a minute they knew that the other had at least three times their speed, and that their escape was quite cut off.

'Turn and double back,' roared Simpson.

Almost in her own length the boat turned and raced for the shore again, the other one after her.

'Over there,' cried Simpson. 'They'll hardly dare to follow us near those rocks. It is our only hope of escape.'

'Can't be done,' said the other man, 'we shall dash ourselves to pieces.' As he spoke he turned for the open sea again, but the chaser turned, too, and it was obvious that they were trapped.

'Out of the way,' cried Simpson, pushing the other man from the wheel. 'I'll get her in somewhere.'

He headed for a little inlet between the rocks near the headland.

'Don't be mad,' shouted the other. 'There's a reef there. Look out!'

Seeing a mad resolve in Simpson's eyes he stood up, and heedless of the enormous wash made by their own speed flung himself overboard. The other boat had turned away and had slowed down as if her occupants knew exactly what was going to happen.

Simpson did not give a glance towards his companion, but leaned forward and switched off his engine. But he was too late. Within a second his racer struck a reef with such violence that the bottom was literally torn right out of her. He was thrown forward with a terrific smash, and then there was an appalling explosion. The force of it was so great that the men in the other boat were almost stunned by it.

In a few seconds there was nothing to be seen of the wrecked boat or Simpson. The other man had miraculously fought his way through the rough water and had been saved from the force of the explosion by the fact that at the moment he was submerged beneath a big wave.

The other boat drew cautiously near, saw him, and hauled him aboard. It was Maclean who dragged him in. He gave one glance at the man's face and then said:

'So you were in it, Samuel Gurney, were you? And I thought you were one that I could trust.'

The day did not end without further excitement, for it

was a long time before Colonel Ridler and Inspector Snelgrove were rescued, and then there was David still missing. There was a great deal of anxiety about him.

Maclean and the Customs men with him, several policemen, and a dozen of the crew sent ashore by Mr Soss and led by the millionaire in person, searched until evening.

Mummy never gave up hope, and in the end Jean suggested taking Chris to search for him. It was Chris who found him. Alan blamed himself for not thinking of that place before.

David was none the worse, and was, in fact, rather proud of the attention he received. He crowed over Michael, and said:

'You aren't the only one to be kidnapped, you see.'

Mr Soss remarked that he had not had such a good day for years. 'It was rare sport,' he said, 'to watch that chase. I'm glad I had that speed-boat handy and could lend it your fellows. I shall be about ten hours late leaving, but it was worth it.'

After all the excitement of the day was over Alan was allowed to be present with Mummy and Auntie and Colonel Ridler, when the Inspector explained everything.

There had, he said, been a gang of smugglers working the district for years, but they were too clever to be caught. Their success was largely due to the fact that they had such good hiding-places for the stuff.

'Your children discovered one in the wreck, then they found the one in Spion Kop, and the eldest boy found the third. It was that third one which was the most important and which we had been longing most particularly to find.'

'Why?' asked Mummy.

'Those glass tubes. They were to be smuggled out of the country somehow. They contained a newly-discovered explosive of a terribly effective nature.'

'I should think so,' said Alan. 'Simpson must have had them with him when he crashed.'

'I didn't see the explosion,' said the Inspector, 'but even

in my dazed condition I felt it right in the heart of the rock.'

'It made the whole house tremble and rock,' said Mummy.

'Yes, it was very terrible stuff, and the Government were frightfully anxious to find out where it had gone. They thought it had reached some foreign war office some while ago. They will be very relieved to know it hasn't.'

'Then who was this man Simpson?' asked the Colonel.

'He was not one of the ordinary smugglers, but he got to know them and used them for his own ends. He paid them well for everything they did for him. He hid the explosive stuff in the wreck at first, according to the man we took from the sea, but he found out that your children had been there, so he moved it.'

'It seems to me, Inspector,' said the Colonel, 'that these children of Mrs Mackenzie's have been the means of breaking up a very nasty gang of unpleasant people.'

'Yes, sir, but this Simpson was the only one among them really a dangerous character. The others were just country and fishing folk who wanted to make a bit of money by doubtful means.'

'Stidson was one of those, I suppose,' said Mrs Mackie.

'Yes, not a bad man at heart, and after he had shut up your little boy he was terribly anxious for you to find him. He said he only did it in a moment of panic.'

'All's well that ends well,' said the Colonel. 'I think we must wish Mrs Mackenzie good night.'

After they had gone Mummy and Auntie stayed talking with Alan for a long while, going over the strange events of this remarkable holiday.

The following morning at breakfast Micky said what was in the minds of all the Mackies:

'We did have adventure after all, didn't we? I wonder if we shall have any more adventures like it when we come again next year.'

Mummy smiled and looked very happy.

'I wonder,' she said.